DATE DUE			
AUG 1 7 1993			
AUG 1 9 1993			
AUG 3 0 1993			
AUG 2 4 1994			

JUL 0 7 1993

The
HAMMER
of GOD

BOOKS BY ARTHUR C. CLARKE

NONFICTION

Ascent to Orbit: A Scientific
  Autobiography
Boy Beneath the Sea
The Challenge of the Sea
The Challenge of the Spaceship
The Coast of Coral
The Exploration of the Moon
The Exploration of Space
The First Five Fathoms
Going into Space
How the World Was One
Indian Ocean Adventure
Indian Ocean Treasure
Interplanetary Flight
The Making of a Moon
Profiles of the Future
The Promise of Space
The Reefs of Taprobane
Report on Planet Three
The Treasure of the Great Reef
The View from Serendip
Voice Across the Sea
Voices from the Sky
1984: Spring

WITH THE EDITORS OF *LIFE*
Man and Space

WITH THE ASTRONAUTS
First on the Moon

WITH ROBERT SILVERBERG
Into Space

WITH CHESLEY BONESTELL
Beyond Jupiter

WITH SIMON WELFARE AND JOHN FAIRLEY
Arthur C. Clarke's Mysterious World
Arthur C. Clarke's World of Strange
  Powers

FICTION

Across the Sea of Stars
Against the Fall of Night
Childhood's End
The City and the Stars
The Deep Range
Dolphin Island
Earthlight
Expedition to Earth
A Fall of Moondust
The Fountains of Paradise
From the Oceans, from the Stars
The Ghost from the Grand Banks
Glide Path
Imperial Earth
Islands in the Sky
The Lost Worlds of 2001
More Than One Universe
Prelude to Mars
Prelude to Space
Reach for Tomorrow
Rendezvous with Rama
The Sands of Mars
The Sentinel
Tales from the "White Hart"
2001: A Space Odyssey
2010: Odyssey Two
2061: Odyssey Three

WITH GENTRY LEE
Cradle
Rama II
The Garden of Rama

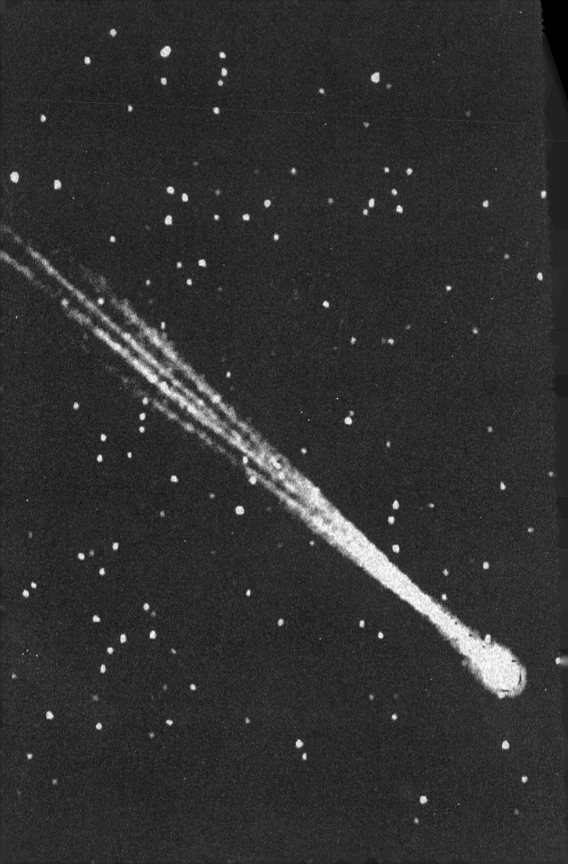

The HAMMER of GOD

ARTHUR C. CLARKE

BANTAM BOOKS

NEW YORK   LONDON   TORONTO   SYDNEY   AUCKLAND

THE HAMMER OF GOD

A Bantam Spectra Book / July 1993

Spectra and the portrayal of a boxed "s" are trademarks of Bantam Books, a division of
Bantam Doubleday Dell Publishing Group, Inc.

Library of Congress Cataloging-in-Publication Data

Clarke, Arthur Charles, 1917–
The hammer of God / Arthur C. Clarke.
p. cm.
ISBN 0-553-09557-9
I. Title.
PR6005.L36H36   1993
823'.914—dc20
93-22096
CIP

Published simultaneously in the United States and Canada

Bantam Books are published by Bantam Books, a division of Bantam Doubleday Dell Publishing Group, Inc. Its trademark, consisting of the words "Bantam Books" and the portrayal
of a rooster, is Registered in U.S. Patent and Trademark Office and in other countries. Marca
Registrada. Bantam Books, 1540 Broadway, New York, New York 10036.

PRINTED IN THE UNITED STATES OF AMERICA
RRH   0 9 8 7 6 5 4 3 2 1

All the events set in the past happened at the times and places
stated: all those set in the future are possible.
And one is certain.
Sooner or later, we will meet Kali.

CONTENTS

VI

VII

Encounter One

OREGON, 1972

It was the size of a small house, weighed nine thousand tons, and was moving at fifty thousand kilometers an hour. As it passed over the Grand Teton National Park, one alert tourist photographed the incandescent fireball and its long vapor trail. In less than two minutes it had sliced through the Earth's atmosphere and returned to space.

The slightest change of orbit during the billions of years it had been circling the sun and it could have descended upon any of the world's great cities—with an explosive force five times more powerful than the bomb that destroyed Hiroshima.

The date was August 10, 1972.

1

OUT
OF
AFRICA

CAPTAIN ROBERT SINGH ENJOYED THESE WALKS THROUGH THE FOR-
est with his little son, Toby. It was, of course, a tamed and
gentle forest, guaranteed to be free of dangerous animals, but
it made an exciting contrast to their last environment in the
Arizona desert. Above all, it was good to be so close to the
ocean, for which all spacers had a deep-seated empathy. Even
here, in this clearing more than a kilometer inland, he could
hear faintly the roar of the monsoon-driven surf against the
outer reef.

"What's *that,* Daddy?" asked the four-year-old, pointing to
a small, hairy face, fringed with white whiskers, peering at
them through a screen of leaves.

"Er—some kind of monkey. Why don't you ask the
Brain?"

"I did. It won't answer."

Another problem, thought Singh. There were times when

he pined for the simple life of his ancestors on the dusty plains of India, though he knew perfectly well that he would have been able to tolerate it only for milliseconds.

"Try again, Toby. Sometimes you speak too quickly— House Central doesn't always recognize your voice. And did you remember to send an image? It can't tell you what *you're* looking at unless it can see it as well."

"Whoops! I forgot."

Singh called for his son's private channel, just in time to catch Central's reply.

"It's a White Colobus, Family Cercopithecidae—"

"Thanks, Brain. Can I play with it?"

"I don't think that's a good idea," Singh interjected hastily. "It could bite. And it probably has fleas. Your robotoys are much nicer."

"Not as nice as Tigrette."

"Though not so much trouble—even now she's house trained, thank goodness. Anyway, it's time to go home." And to see what progress, he added to himself, Freyda is making in *her* problems with Central . . .

Ever since the Skylift Service had set the house down in Africa, there had been a succession of glitches. The latest, and potentially most serious, was with the food recycling system. Although it was guaranteed to be fail-safe so that the risk of actual poisoning was astronomically small, there had been a curious metallic taste to the filet mignon the night before. Freyda had suggested wryly that they might have to revert to a life of pre-electronic hunter-gatherers, cooking their food over wood fires. Her sense of humor was sometimes a little bizarre: the very idea of eating natural meat hacked from dead animals was, of course, utterly revolting. . . .

"Can't we go down to the beach?"

Toby, who had spent most of his life surrounded by sand, was fascinated by the sea; he could not quite believe that it was possible for so much water to exist in one place. As soon as the North East Monsoon slackened, his father would take him out to the reef and show him the wonders that were now hidden by the angry waves.

"Let's see what Mother has to say."

"Mother says it's time for you both to come home. Have you two men forgotten we've visitors coming this afternoon? And Toby—your room is a *mess*. Time *you* cleaned it up—not left it to Dorcas."

"But I programmed her—"

"No arguments. Home—*both* of you!"

Toby's mouth started to pucker in an all-too-familiar response. But there were times when discipline took precedence over love: Captain Singh cradled Toby in his arms and started to walk back to the house with his gently wriggling bundle. Toby was too heavy to carry very far, but his struggles quickly subsided and his father was soon glad enough to let him proceed under his own power.

The home shared by Robert Singh, Freyda Carroll, their son, Toby, his beloved minitiger, and assorted robots would have seemed surprisingly small to a visitor from an earlier century—a cottage rather than a house. But in this case appearances were extremely deceptive, for most of the rooms were multifunctional and could be transformed on command. Furniture would metamorphose, walls and ceiling would vanish to be replaced by vistas of land or sky—or even space, convincing enough to deceive anyone except an astronaut.

The complex of central dome and four hemicylindrical wings was not, Singh had to admit, very pleasing to the eye, and it looked distinctly out of place in this jungle clearing. But it fitted perfectly the description "A machine for living in"; Singh had spent virtually all his adult life in such machines, often in zero gravity. He would not feel comfortable in any other environment.

The front door folded upward, and a golden blur erupted toward them. Arms outstretched, Toby rushed forward to greet Tigrette.

But they never met; for this reality was thirty years earlier and half a billion kilometers away.

2
RENDEZVOUS
WITH KALI

As the neural playback came to an end, sound, vision, the scent of unknown flowers, and the gentle touch of the wind on his decades-younger skin faded and Captain Singh was back in his cabin aboard the space-tug *Goliath,* while Toby and his mother remained on a world he could never revisit. Years in space—and neglect of the mandatory zero-gee exercises—had so weakened him that he could now walk only on the Moon and Mars. Gravity had exiled him from the planet of his birth.

"One hour to rendezvous, Captain," said the quiet but insistent voice of David, as *Goliath*'s central computer had been inevitably named. "Active Mode as requested. Time to leave your memochips and come back to the real world."

Goliath's human commander felt a wave of sadness sweep over him as the final image from his lost past dissolved into a featureless, simmering mist of white noise. Too swift a transi-

tion from one reality to another was a good recipe for schizo-
phrenia, and Captain Singh always eased the shock with the
most soothing sound he knew—waves falling gently on a
beach, with sea gulls crying in the distance. It was yet another
memory of a life he had lost, and of a peaceful past now
replaced by a terrifying present.

For a few more moments he delayed facing his awesome
responsibility. Then he sighed, and removed the neural input
cap that fitted snugly over his skull. Like all spacers, Captain
Singh belonged to the "Bald is Beautiful" school, if only because hairpieces were a nuisance in zero gravity. The social
historians were still staggered by the fact that one invention,
the portable "Brainman," could change the appearance of the
human race within a single decade—and restore the ancient
art of wigmaking to the status of a major industry.

"Captain," said David. "I know you're there. Or do you
want me to take over?"

It was an old joke inspired by all the insane computers in
the fiction and movies of the early electronic age. David had a
surprisingly good sense of humor: he was, after all, a Legal
Person (nonhuman) under the famous Hundredth Amendment, and shared—or surpassed—almost all the attributes of
his creators. But there were whole sensory and emotional areas that he could not enter. It had been felt unnecessary to
equip him with the senses of smell and taste, though it would
have been easy to do so. And all his attempts at telling dirty
stories were such disastrous failures that he had abandoned
the genre.

"All right, David," retorted the captain. "I'm still in
charge." He removed the mask from his eyes, wiped away the
tears that had somehow accumulated, and turned reluctantly
toward the viewport. There, hanging in space before him, was
Kali.

It looked harmless enough—just another small asteroid,

shaped so exactly like a peanut that the resemblance was almost comical. A few large impact craters, and hundreds of tiny ones, were scattered at random over its charcoal-black surface. There were no visual clues to give any sense of scale, but Singh knew its dimensions by heart: 1295 meters maximum length, 656 meters minimum width; Kali would fit easily into many city parks.

No wonder that, even now, most of mankind could still not believe that it was the instrument of doom. Or, as the Chrislamic Fundamentalists were calling it, "The Hammer of God."

•   •   •

IT HAD OFTEN BEEN SUGGESTED THAT *GOLIATH*'S BRIDGE HAD BEEN copied from the starship *Enterprise:* after a century and a half, *Star Trek* was still affectionately revived from time to time. It was a reminder of the naive dawn of the Space Age, when men dreamed it might be possible to defy the laws of physics and race across the Universe more swiftly than light itself. But no way of avoiding the speed limit set by Einstein had been discovered—and although "wormholes in space" had been proved to exist, nothing even as large as an atomic nucleus could pass through them. Yet despite this, the dream of *really* conquering the interstellar gulfs had not wholly died.

Kali filled the main view-screen. No magnification was needed, for *Goliath* was hovering only two hundred meters above its ancient, battered surface. And now, for the first time in its existence, it had visitors.

Though it was a commander's privilege to take the first step on a virgin world, Captain Singh had delegated the landing to three crew members more experienced in extravehicular activities. He was anxious not to waste any time: most of the human race was watching, and waiting for the verdict that would decide the fate of the Earth.

It is impossible to walk on the smaller asteroids; gravity is so feeble that a careless explorer can easily achieve escape velocity and go heading off on an independent orbit. One member of the contact team was therefore wearing a self-propelled hard suit fitted with external grasping arms. The other two rode on a small space-sled that could easily have been mistaken for one of its Arctic analogues.

Captain Singh and the dozen officers gathered around him on *Goliath*'s bridge knew better than to bother the EVA team with unnecessary questions or advice, unless some emergency arose.

The sled had now touched down on the summit of a large boulder several times its own size, blasting away a surprisingly impressive cloud of dust as it did so.

"Touchdown, *Goliath*! Can see the bare rock now. Shall we anchor?"

"Looks as good a place as any. Go ahead."

"Deploying drill . . . seems to be going in easily . . . won't it be great if we strike oil?"

There were a few low groans on the bridge. Such feeble jokes served to relieve tension, and Singh encouraged them. Ever since rendezvous there had been a subtle change in the crew's morale, with unpredictable swings between gloom and juvenile humor—"whistling past the graveyard" as the ship's physician had privately labeled it. She had already prescribed tranquilizers for one mild case of manic-depressive symptoms. It would grow steadily worse in the weeks and months ahead.

"Erecting the antenna—deploying the radio beacon—how are the signals?"

"Loud and clear."

"Good. Now Kali won't be able to hide."

Not, of course, that there was the slightest danger of losing Kali—as had happened many times in the past with asteroids that had been poorly observed. No orbit had ever been computed with greater care, but some uncertainty still existed. There was still a slim chance that the Hammer of God might miss the anvil.

Now the giant radio telescopes on Earth and lunar Farside were waiting to receive the pulses from the beacon, timed to a thousandth of a millionth of a millionth of a second. It would be more than twenty minutes before they reached their destination, creating an invisible measuring rod that would define Kali's orbit to within a matter of centimeters.

A few seconds later, the SPACEGUARD computers would give their verdict of life or death: but it would be almost an hour before the word got back to *Goliath*.

The first waiting period had begun.

TUNGUSKA, SIBERIA, 1908

The cosmic iceberg came in from the direction of the sun, so no one saw its approach until the sky exploded. Seconds later, the shock wave flattened two thousand square kilometers of pine forest, and the loudest sound since the eruption of Krakatoa began to circle the world.

Had the cometary fragment been delayed a mere two hours on its age-long journey, the ten-megaton blast would have obliterated Moscow and changed the course of history.

The date was June 30, 1908.

SPACEGUARD

SPACEGUARD had been one of the last projects of the
legendary NASA, back at the close of the Twentieth Century.
Its initial objective had been modest enough: to make as
complete a survey as possible of the asteroids and comets that
crossed the orbit of Earth, and to determine if any were a
potential threat. The project's name—taken from an obscure
Twentieth-Century science-fiction novel—was somewhat
misleading; critics were fond of pointing out that
"Spacewatch" or "Spacewarn" would have been much more
appropriate.

With a total budget seldom exceeding ten million dollars a
year, a worldwide network of telescopes—most of them
operated by skilled amateurs—was established by 2000. Sixty-
one years later, the spectacular return of Halley's Comet
encouraged more funding, and the great fireball of 2079—
luckily impacting in mid-Atlantic—gave SPACEGUARD

additional prestige. By the end of the century it had located more than a million asteroids, and the survey was believed to be 90 percent complete. However, it would have to be continued indefinitely: there was always a chance that some intruder might come rushing in from the uncharted outer reaches of the Solar System.

As did Kali, detected in late 2109 as it fell sunward past the orbit of Saturn.

3
STONES
FROM THE
SKY

"There's never been so much talent gathered here in the White House since Thomas Jefferson dined alone."
—PRESIDENT JOHN KENNEDY TO A DELEGATION
OF UNITED STATES SCIENTISTS

"I would sooner believe that two Yankee professors lied than that stones could fall from the sky."
—PRESIDENT THOMAS JEFFERSON ON HEARING A REPORT
OF A METEORITE FALL IN NEW ENGLAND

"Meteorites don't fall on the Earth. They fall on the sun —and the Earth gets in the way."
—JOHN W. CAMPBELL

THAT STONES COULD INDEED FALL FROM THE SKY WAS WELL KNOWN in the ancient world, though there might be disagreement as to which particular gods had dropped them. And not only stones, but the precious metal Iron. Before the invention of smelting, meteorites were a main source of this valuable element: no wonder that they became sacred, and were frequently worshiped.

But the more enlightened thinkers of the Eighteenth Century's "Age of Reason" knew better than to believe such superstitious nonsense. Indeed, the French Academy of Science passed a resolution explaining that meteorites were of completely terrestrial origin. If any *appeared* to come from the sky, it was because they were the result of lightning strikes—a perfectly understandable error. So the curators of Europe's museums threw away the worthless rocks their ignorant predecessors had patiently collected.

By one of the most delightful ironies in the history of science, just a few years after the French Academy's pronouncement, a massive shower of meteorites descended a few kilometers outside Paris in the presence of impeccable witnesses. The Academy had to make a hasty recantation.

Even so, it was not until the dawn of the Space Age that the magnitude, and potential importance, of meteorites was recognized. For decades scientists doubted—and even denied—that they were responsible for any major formations on Earth. Almost incredibly, until well into the Twentieth Century some geologists believed that Arizona's famous "Meteor Crater" was misnamed—they argued that it had a volcanic origin! Not until space probes had shown that the Moon and most of the smaller bodies in the Solar System had been subjected to a cosmic bombardment for ages was the debate finally resolved.

As soon as they started to look for them—particularly with the new vision provided by cameras in orbit—geologists found impact craters everywhere. The reason they were not much more common was now obvious: all the ancient ones had been destroyed by weathering. And some were so enormous that they could not be seen from the ground, or even from the air: their scale could be grasped only from space.

All this was very interesting to geologists, but too remote from ordinary human affairs to excite the general public. Then, thanks to Nobel Laureate Luis Alvarez and his son, Walter, the minor science of meteoritics suddenly became front-page news.

The abrupt—at least on the astronomical time-scale—disappearance of the great dinosaurs, after dominating the Earth for more than a hundred million years, had always been a major mystery. Many explanations had been advanced, some plausible, some frankly ludicrous. A change of climate was the simplest and most obvious answer, and had inspired one classic work of art—the brilliant "Rite of Spring" sequence in Walt Disney's masterpiece *Fantasia.*

But that explanation was not really satisfactory because it posed more questions than it answered. If the climate changed—what caused that change? There were so many theories, none really convincing, that scientists began to look elsewhere.

In 1980 Luis and Walter Alvarez, searching the geological record, announced that they had solved the long-standing mystery. In a narrow layer of rock marking the boundary between the Cretaceous and Tertiary eras, they found evidence of a global catastrophe.

The dinosaurs had been murdered: and they knew the weapon.

GULF OF MEXICO
65,000,000 BP

It came in vertically, punching a hole ten kilometers wide through the atmosphere, generating temperatures so high that the air itself started to burn. When it hit the ground, rock turned to liquid and spread outward in mountainous waves, not freezing until it had formed a crater two hundred kilometers across.

That was only the beginning of disaster: now the real tragedy began.

Nitric oxides rained from the air, turning the sea to acid. Clouds of soot from incinerated forests darkened the sky, hiding the sun for months. Worldwide, the temperature dropped precipitously, killing off most of the plants and animals that had survived the initial cataclysm. Though some species would linger on for millennia, the reign of the great reptiles was finally over.

The clock of Evolution had been reset; the countdown to Man had begun.

The date was, very approximately, 65,000,000 Before Present.

4
DEATH
SENTENCE

*"Given for one instant an intelligence that could
comprehend all the forces by which nature is animated
. . . an intelligence sufficiently vast to submit these data
to analysis . . . it would embrace in the same formula
the movements of the greatest bodies in the universe
and those of the lightest atom; for it, nothing would be
uncertain and the future, as the past, would be present
to its eyes."*

—PIERRE-SIMON DE LAPLACE, 1814

ROBERT SINGH HAD LITTLE PATIENCE WITH PHILOSOPHICAL SPECULA-
tions, but when he first encountered the great French mathematician's words in an astronomy textbook, he felt something
close to horror. However improbable an "intelligence sufficiently vast" might be, the very idea of its possibility was
frightful. Was "free will," which Singh fondly imagined he

possessed, no more than an illusion since his every act could be predetermined, at least in principle?

He was vastly relieved when he learned how the Laplacian nightmare had been exorcised by the development of Chaos Theory in the late Twentieth Century.

It was then realized that not even the future of a single atom—let alone the whole Universe—could be predicted with perfect accuracy. To do so would require that its initial location and its velocity would have to be known with *infinite* precision. Any error in the millionth or billionth or centillionth place would ultimately build up, until reality and theory no longer bore the slightest resemblance.

Yet some events could be predicted with absolute confidence, at least over periods of time that were long by human standards. The movements of the planets under the gravitational field of the sun—and of each other—was the classic example, to which Laplace devoted his genius when he was not discussing philosophy with Napoleon. Although the long-term stability of the Solar System could not be guaranteed, the positions of the planets could be calculated for tens of thousands of years into the future, within very small limits of error.

The future of Kali needed to be known only for a matter of months, and the allowable error was the diameter of Earth. Now that the radio beacon implanted on the asteroid had allowed its orbit to be computed with the necessary precision, there was no further room for uncertainty—or hope. . . .

Not that Robert Singh had ever allowed himself much hope. The message that David reported to him, as soon as it arrived by tight infrared beam from the lunar relay station, was just what he had expected.

"SPACEWATCH computers report that Kali will hit Earth in 241 days 13 hours 05 minutes, plus or minus 20 minutes. Ground zero still being determined: probably Pacific area."

So Kali would land in the ocean; that would do nothing to reduce the extent of the global catastrophe. It might even make it worse, when a kilometer-high wave swept to the foothills of the Himalayas.

"I've acknowledged," said David. "There's another message coming through."

"I know."

It could not have been more than a minute, but it seemed like an eternity.

"SPACEGUARD Control to *Goliath*. You are authorized to begin Operation ATLAS immediately."

5
ATLAS

THE TASK OF THE MYTHOLOGICAL ATLAS WAS TO STOP THE HEAVENS from crashing down upon Earth. That of the ATLAS propulsion module that *Goliath* carried was much simpler. It had merely to hold back a very small portion of the sky.

Assembled on Deimos, the outer satellite of Mars, ATLAS was little more than a set of rocket engines attached to propellant tanks holding two hundred thousand tons of liquid hydrogen. Though its fusion drive could generate less thrust than the primitive missile that had carried Yuri Gagarin into space, it could run continuously not merely for minutes, but for weeks. Even so, its effect on a body the size of Kali would be trivial—a velocity change of a few centimeters per second. But that should be sufficient if all went well.

It seemed a pity that the men who had fought so hard for—and against—Project ATLAS would never know the outcome of their efforts.

6
THE SENATOR

Senator George Ledstone (Independent, W. America) had one public eccentricity, and, he cheerfully admitted, one secret vice. He always wore massive horn-rimmed spectacles (nonfunctional, of course) because they had an intimidating effect on uncooperative witnesses, few of whom had ever encountered such a novelty in this age of instant laser eye surgery.

His "secret vice"—perfectly well known to everyone—was rifle shooting on a standard Olympic range set up in the corridors of a long-abandoned missile silo near Mount Cheyenne. Ever since the demilitarization of Planet Earth, such activities had been frowned upon, if not actively discouraged.

The senator approved the U.N. resolution, triggered by the mass slaughters of the Twentieth Century, which banned the ownership by States *or* individuals of all weapons that could injure more than the single person targeted. Nevertheless he pooh-poohed the "World Saver's" famous slogan: "Guns are the crutches of the impotent."

"Not for me," he retorted during one of his countless interviews. (The media people loved him.) "I've got two kids, and would have a dozen if the law allowed. I'm not ashamed to admit that I love a good rifle—it's a work of art. When you give that second pressure on the trigger, and see you've hit the bull's-eye—well, there's no feeling like it. And if marksmanship is a substitute for sex, I'll settle for both."

What the senator *did* draw the line at, however, was hunting.

"Of course, that was okay when there was no other way of getting meat—but to shoot defenseless animals for sport—now, that really *is* sick! I did it once, when I was a kid. A squirrel—luckily it wasn't a protected species—ran onto our lawn, and I couldn't resist the temptation. . . . Dad gave me a whopping, but it wasn't necessary. I'll never forget the mess my bullet made."

There was no doubt that Senator Ledstone was an original; it seemed to run in the family. His grandmother had been a colonel in the dreaded Beverly Hills Militia, whose skirmishes with the L.A. Irregulars had spawned endless psychodramas in every medium from old-fashioned ballet to memnochip. And his grandfather had been one of the most notorious bootleggers of the Twenty-First Century. Before he was killed in a shootout with the Medicops Canadien during an ingenious attempt to smuggle a kiloton of tobacco *up* Niagara Falls, it was estimated that "Smoky" Ledstone had been responsible for at least twenty million deaths.

Ledstone was quite unrepentant about his grandfather, whose sensational demise had triggered the repeal of the late USA's third, and most disastrous, attempt at Prohibition. He argued that responsible adults should be allowed to commit suicide in any way they pleased—by alcohol, cocaine, or even tobacco—as long as they did not kill innocent bystanders during the process. Certainly Grandpop was a saint compared to the advertising tycoons who, until their high-priced lawyers could no longer keep them out of jail, had managed to fatally addict a substantial fraction of the human species.

The Commonwealth of American States still held its General Assembly in Washington, in surroundings that would have been perfectly familiar to generations of viewers—though anyone born in the Twentieth Century would have been extremely perplexed by the procedures and forms of address. Yet many committees and subcommittees still kept their original names, because most of the problems of administration are eternal.

It was as chairman of the CAS Appropriations Committee that Senator Ledstone first encountered Spaceguard Phase II—and was outraged. It was true that the global economy was in good shape; since the collapse of communism and capitalism—now so long ago that both events seemed simultaneous—the skillful application of Chaos Theory by World Bank mathematicians had broken the old cycle of booms and busts, and averted (so far) the Final Depression predicted by many pessimists. Nevertheless, the senator argued that money could be much better spent on terra firma—especially on his favorite project, reconstructing what was left of California after the Superquake.

When Ledstone had twice vetoed the proposal to fund Spaceguard Phase II, everyone agreed that no one on Earth would make him change his mind. They had not reckoned with someone from Mars.

7

THE
SCIENTIST

THE RED PLANET WAS NO LONGER QUITE SO RED, THOUGH THE process of greening it had barely begun. Concentrating on the problems of survival, the colonists (they hated the word, and were already saying proudly "we Martians") had little energy left over for art or science. But the lightning-flash of genius strikes where it will, and the greatest theoretical physicist of the century was born under the bubble-domes of Port Lowell.

Like Einstein, to whom he was often compared, Carlos Mendoza was an excellent musician; he owned the only saxophone on Mars, and was a skilled performer on that antique instrument. He also shared Einstein's self-deprecating wit: when his gravitational-wave predictions were dramatically verified, his only comment was "Well, that disposes of the Big Bang Theory, Version 5—at least until Wednesday."

Carlos could have received his Nobel Prize on Mars, as

everyone expected. But he loved surprises and practical jokes: so he appeared in Stockholm looking like a knight in high-tech armor, wearing one of the powered exoskeletons developed for paraplegics. With this mechanical assistance he could function almost unhandicapped in an environment that would otherwise have quickly killed him.

Needless to say, when the ceremony was over, Carlos was bombarded with invitations to scientific and social functions. Among the few he was able to accept was an appearance before the CAS Appropriations Committee where he made an unforgettable impression:

SENATOR LEDSTONE: Professor Mendoza—have you ever heard of Chicken Little?

PROFESSOR MENDOZA: I'm afraid not, Mr. Chairman.

SENATOR LEDSTONE: Well, he was a character in a fairy tale who rushed around crying "The sky is falling! The sky is falling!" He reminds me of some of your colleagues—I'd appreciate your views on Project Spaceguard—I'm sure you know what I'm talking about.

PROFESSOR MENDOZA: Indeed I do, Mr. Chairman. I live on a world that still bears the scars of a thousand meteor impacts—some of them *hundreds* of kilometers across. Once they were equally common on Earth, but wind and rain—something we don't yet have on Mars, though we're working on it!—have worn them away. You still have one pristine example, though, in Arizona.

SENATOR LEDSTONE: I know—I know—the Spaceguarders are always pointing to Meteor Crater. How seriously should we take their warnings?

PROFESSOR MENDOZA: Very seriously, Mr. Chairman. Sooner or later there's bound to be another major impact. It's not my field, but I'll look up the statistics for you.

SENATOR LEDSTONE: I'm *drowning* in statistics—but I'd value your considered opinion. And I appreciate your appearance at such short notice, especially as you have an appointment with President Windsor in a few hours.

PROFESSOR MENDOZA: Thank you, Mr. Chairman.

Senator Ledstone was impressed, and indeed charmed, by the young scientist, but not yet convinced; what changed his mind was not a matter of logic. For Carlos Mendoza never made that appointment in Buckingham Palace. On his way to London he was killed in a bizarre accident when the control system of his exoskeleton malfunctioned.

Ledstone immediately dropped his opposition to SPACE-GUARD, and voted to release funds for the next phase. When he was a very old man he said to one of his aides: "They tell me we'll soon be able to take Mendoza's brain out of that tank of liquid nitrogen and talk to it through a computer interface. I wonder what it's been thinking about all these years. . . ."

II

8
CHANCE
AND
NECESSITY

*THIS STORY HAS BEEN TOLD IN THE BAZAARS OF IRAQ FOR CENTURIES,
and is really very sad: therefore do not laugh.*

*Abdul Hassan was a famous maker of carpets in the reign of
the Great Caliph, who much admired his craftsmanship. But
one day, as he was presenting his wares at the Court, a frightful
catastrophe occurred.*

*When Abdul bowed low before Haroun al Rashid, he broke
wind.*

*That night, the carpet-maker closed his shop, piled his most
precious wares upon a single camel, and left Baghdad. For years
he wandered, changing his name but not his profession, over
the lands of Syria, Persia, and Iraq. He prospered, but always he
yearned for the beloved city of his birth.*

*He was an old man when at last he felt sure that everyone
had forgotten his disgrace, and it was safe to turn homeward
again. The night was falling when the minarets of Baghdad*

came in sight, so he decided to rest at a convenient hostel before entering the city in the morning.

The innkeeper was talkative and friendly, so Abdul was delighted to ply him for news of all that had occurred during his long absence. They were both laughing over one of the court scandals when Abdul asked casually: "When did that *happen?"*

The innkeeper paused in thought, then scratched his head.

"I'm not sure of the date," he said, "but it was about five years after Abdul Hassan farted."

So the carpet-maker never did return to Baghdad.

• • •

THE MOST TRIFLING EVENTS CAN, IN A MERE MOMENT OF TIME, TOtally change the course of a man's life. And often it is not possible, even at the end, to decide whether the change was for better or worse. Who knows: Abdul's involuntary performance might well have saved his life. Had he remained in Baghdad, he could have become the victim of an assassin—or, far worse, have incurred the disfavor of the caliph, and consequently the skilled services of his executioners.

When twenty-five-year-old Cadet Robert Singh had started his final semester at the Aristarchus Institute of Space Technology—usually known as Arri Tech—he would have laughed if anyone had suggested that he would soon become an Olympics competitor. Like all Moon residents who wished to keep the option of returning to Earth, he had religiously carried out his hi-gee exercises in the Arri Tech centrifuge. Though they were boring, the time was not completely wasted, as he spent most of it plugged into his study programs.

Then one day the Dean of Engineering summoned him into his office—a sufficiently unusual event to alarm any finals student. But he appeared to be in a good mood, so Singh relaxed.

"Mister Singh—your academic record is satisfactory, though not brilliant. But I don't want to talk to you about that.

"You may not be aware of the fact, but according to the medical readouts, you have an unusually good mass/energy ratio. So we'd like you to go into training for the upcoming Olympics."

Singh was startled and not particularly pleased. His first reaction was "How will I ever find the time?" But almost at once a second thought flashed through his mind. Any deficiencies in his academic record might well be overlooked if there were compensating athletic achievements. There was a long and honorable tradition to this effect.

"Thank you, sir—I'm very flattered. I suppose I'll have to move to the Astrodome."

The three-kilometer-wide roof over a crater near the eastern wall of Plato enclosed the largest single airspace on the Moon, and had become a popular venue for human-powered flight. There had been talk for some years of making this an Olympics event, but the IOC had not been able to decide whether contestants should use wings or props. Singh would be happy with either—he had tried both, briefly, on a visit to the Astrodome complex.

He was due for another surprise.

"You won't be flying, Mister Singh. You'll be *running*. On the open moonscape. Probably across the Sinus Iridum."

• • •

FREYDA CARROLL HAD BEEN ON THE MOON FOR ONLY A FEW weeks, and now that the novelty had worn off, she wished she were back on Earth.

In the first place, she could not become accustomed to the one-sixth gravity. Some visitors never did grow used to it—

they either hopped like kangaroos, occasionally hitting the ceiling, and making little forward progress—or shuffled cautiously along, pausing between each step before they took the next. No wonder that the locals called them "Earthworms."

As a geology student, Freyda also found the Moon a disappointment. Oh, it had geology—well, selenology—enough to occupy anyone for a hundred lifetimes. But the interesting bits of the Moon were hard to get at; you couldn't go wandering round with hammer and pocket mass-spectrometer as you did on Earth, but had to put on spacesuits (which Freyda hated) or sit in a rover and control Remotes—which was almost as bad.

She had hoped that the endless tunnels and underground facilities of Arri Tech would provide cross-sections of the Moon's upper hundred meters, but no such luck. The high-powered lasers that had done the excavating had fused rock and regolith to give a featureless, mirror-smooth finish. No wonder it was easy to get lost in the dull uniformity of tunnels and corridors; myriads of signs like

NO ADMISSION UNDER ANY CIRCUMSTANCES!
ROBOTS CLASS 2 ONLY!
CLOSED FOR REPAIRS
CAUTION—BAD AIR—USE RESPIRATOR

did not encourage the sort of exploration that Freyda enjoyed on Earth.

She was lost—as usual—when she pushed open a door which promised access to MAIN SUBBASEMENT #3, and launched herself cautiously through it. But not cautiously enough.

Almost at once she was hit by a large, rapidly moving object, and sent spinning to one side of the wide corridor she had just entered. For a moment she was completely disoriented, and it was several seconds before she picked herself up and checked for injuries.

Nothing seemed broken, but she suspected that there would very soon be a painful bruise on her left side. Then, more angry than alarmed, she looked around for the projectile that had caused the damage.

An entity that might have escaped from an ancient comic strip was coming slowly toward her. It was obviously human, and encased in a glittering silver suit as closely fitting as a ballet dancer's leotard. The wearer's head was concealed in a bubble that looked disproportionately large: Freyda could see only her own distorted figure in its mirror surface.

She waited for an explanation or apology (but, on second thought, perhaps she *should* have been a little more careful . . .). As the figure approached her, holding out its arms in a supplicating manner, she heard a muffled and barely intelligible male voice say:

"I'm very sorry—hope you weren't hurt, I thought no one ever came here."

Freyda tried to see into the helmet, but it completely concealed the wearer's face.

"I'm all right—I *think*."

The voice from the spacesuit (for what else could it be, though she had never seen one remotely like it?) sounded rather attractive as well as contrite, and her annoyance quickly evaporated.

"I hope I've not injured you—or damaged your equipment."

Now Mr. X was so close that his suit was almost touching her, and Freyda could tell that he was studying her intently. It seemed unfair that he could see her, while she had no idea what he looked like. She suddenly realized that she very much wished to know. . . .

. . . .In the Arri Tech cafeteria a few hours later, she was not disappointed. Bob Singh still seemed embarrassed by the incident, though not entirely for the reason that might have been expected. As soon as Freyda had assured him that she was probably going to survive, he turned to a subject that was obviously of more immediate importance.

"We're still experimenting with the suit," he explained, "and running tests on the life-support system—indoors, where it's safe! Next week, if everything works, we'll try it outside. But we have a problem with—ah—security. Clavius is definitely entering a team, and Tsiolkovski on Farside is thinking about it. So are MIT and CalTech and Gagarin—but no one takes them seriously. They don't have the know-how —and how could they do any proper training on Earth?"

Freyda's interest in athletics was almost zero, but she was rapidly warming to the subject. Or at least to Robert Singh.

"You're afraid that someone will copy your design?"

"Exactly. And if it's as successful as we hope, it may cause a revolution in EVA gear—at least for short-duration missions. We'd like Arri Tech to get the credit. After more than a hundred years, spacesuits are still clumsy and uncomfortable. You know the old joke 'I wouldn't be seen dead in one.' "

The joke was indeed an old one, but Freyda laughed dutifully. Then she became serious, and looked straight into her new friend's eyes.

"I hope," she said, "you're not going to take any risks."

It was then that she knew that for only the second or third time in her life, she had fallen in love.

• • •

THE DEAN OF ASTRONAUTICS, ALREADY SOMEWHAT DESPONDENT BEcause his spy at MIT had just been ceremonially dumped in the Charles River, was not too happy about Robert Singh's new roommate.

"I'll make sure she's sent on a field trip at least three days before the race," he threatened.

But on further thought, he relented. In determining an athlete's performance, psychological factors were just as important as physiological ones.

Freyda would not be banished before the Marathon.

9
BAY
OF
RAINBOWS

THE GRACEFUL ARC OF THE BAY OF RAINBOWS IS ONE OF THE LOVE-
liest of all lunar formations. Three hundred kilometers across,
it is the surviving half of a typical crater-plain, whose entire
northern wall was washed away three billion years ago by a
flood of lava sweeping down from the Sea of Rains. The remaining semicircle, which the lava could not breach, is termi-
nated at its western end by the kilometer-high Promontory
Heraclides, a group of hills that at certain times creates a brief
and beautiful illusion. When the Moon is ten days old, wax-
ing toward full, Promontory Heraclides greets the dawn, and
even in the smallest of Earth-based telescopes it appears for a
few hours like the profile of a young woman, hair streaming
toward the west. Then, as the sun rises higher, the pattern of
shadows changes, and the Moon Maiden disappears.

But there was no sun now, as the contestants for the first
Lunar Marathon gathered at the foothills of the Promontory.

Indeed, it was almost local midnight: the Full Earth hung halfway down the southern sky, flooding all this land with an electric-blue radiance fifty times more brilliant than the Full Moon can ever cast upon the Earth. It also drove the stars from the sky; only Jupiter was palely visible low in the west, if one looked for it carefully.

Robert Singh had never been in the public eye before, yet even knowing that three worlds and a dozen satellites were watching did not make him feel particularly nervous. As he had told Freyda twenty-four hours earlier, he had complete confidence in his equipment.

"Well, you've just demonstrated *that,*" she said dreamily.

"Thank you. But I've promised the dean it's the last time until after the race."

"You haven't!"

"Not really; let's say it was—well, an unspoken gentleman's agreement."

Freyda became suddenly serious.

"I hope you win, of course—but I'm more worried that something may go wrong. You can't have had enough time to test that suit properly."

That was perfectly true, but Singh was not going to alarm Freyda by admitting it. Yet even if there was a systems failure —always possible, no matter how much testing one did in advance—there would be no real danger. A small armada of lunar rovers was accompanying them—observation cars containing media people, moonjeeps with cheerleaders and coaches. Most important of all, an ambulance crew, with recompression chamber, would never be more than a few hundred meters away.

As he was being kitted up in the Arri Tech van, Singh wondered which competitor would need to be rescued first. Most of them had met only a few hours earlier, and had exchanged the usual insincere good-luck greetings. There had been eleven entrants originally, but four had dropped out, leaving Arri Tech, Gagarin, Clavius, Tsiolkovski, Goddard, CalTech, and MIT. The runner from MIT—a dark horse named Robert Steel—had not yet arrived, and would be disqualified if he did not turn up within the next ten minutes. That might be a piece of deliberate gamesmanship designed to confuse the competition, or to prevent too close an examination of his space gear—not that it would make much difference at this late stage.

"How's your breathing?" asked Singh's coach when the helmet had been sealed.

"Quite normal."

"Well, you're not exerting yourself at the moment—the regulator can increase O_2 flow up to ten times, if you need it. Now, let's get you into the airlock, and check your mobility. . . ."

"The team from MIT has just arrived," announced the Interplanetary Olympics Committee's observer over the public circuit. "The Marathon will begin in fifteen minutes."

• • •

"PLEASE CONFIRM ALL SYSTEMS GO," THE STARTER'S VOICE WHISpered in Robert Singh's ear. "Number One?"

"OK."

"Number Two?"

"Yes."

"Number Three?"

"No problem."

But there was no response from CalTech's Number Four. She was walking, very clumsily, away from the starting line.

That leaves only six of us, thought Singh, feeling a brief flash of sympathy. What bad luck to have come all the way from Earth, only to have an equipment failure at the last moment! But proper testing would have been impossible down there; no simulator would have been large enough. Here it was only necessary to step out through the airlock to find enough vacuum to satisfy anyone.

"Beginning the countdown. Ten, nine, eight . . ."

This was not one of those events that could be won or lost at the starting line. Singh waited until well after "zero," carefully estimating his launch angle, before taking off.

A lot of mathematics had gone into this; almost a millisecond of Arri Tech computer time had been devoted to the problem. The Moon's one-sixth gravity was the most important factor, but by no means the only one. The stiffness of his suit—optimum rate of oxygen intake—heat load—fatigue—all these had to be taken into consideration. And it had first been necessary to settle a long-standing debate, going back to the days of the very first men on the Moon: which was better, hopping or long-jumping?

Both worked quite well, but there was no precedent for what he was attempting now. Until today, all spacesuits had been bulky affairs that restricted mobility and added so much mass to the wearer that it required an effort to start moving, and sometimes an equal effort to stop. But this suit was very different.

Robert Singh had tried to explain those differences—without giving away any trade secrets—during one of the inevitable media interviews before the race.

"How could we make it so light?" he had answered to the first question. "Well, it's not designed for use in daytime."

"Why does that matter?"

"It doesn't need a heat-rejection system. The sun can pump more than a kilowatt into you. That's why we're racing at night."

"Oh. I was wondering about that. But won't you get *too* cold? Doesn't the lunar night get a couple of hundred degrees below zero?"

Singh managed to avoid smiling at such a simple-minded question.

"Your body generates all the heat you need, even on the Moon. And if you're running a marathon—*much* more than you need."

"But can you really *run,* wrapped up like a mummy?"

"Just wait and see!"

He had spoken confidently enough in the security of the studio. But now, standing out on the barren lunar plain, that phrase "like a mummy" came back to haunt him. It was not the most cheerful of comparisons.

He consoled himself with the thought that it was not really very accurate; he was not wrapped up in bandages, but sheathed in two body-tight garments—one active, one passive. The inner one, made of cotton, enclosed him from neck to ankle, and carried a closely packed network of narrow, porous tubes, to carry away perspiration and excess heat. Over that was the tough but extremely flexible protective outer suit, made of a rubberlike material, and fastened by a ring-seal to a helmet that gave 180-degree visibility. When Singh had asked "Why not all-around vision?" he was told firmly "When you're running—never look back."

Well, now was the moment of truth. Using both legs together, he launched himself upward at a shallow angle, deliberately making as little effort as possible. Yet within two seconds he had reached the apex of his trajectory and was traveling parallel to the lunar surface, about four meters above it. That would be a new record on Earth, where the high jump had been stuck at just under three meters for half a century.

For a moment time slowed down to a crawl. He was aware of the great, glowing plain stretching out to the unbroken curve of the horizon: the Earthlight slanting over his right shoulder gave the extraordinary illusion that the Sinus Iridum was covered with snow. All the other runners were ahead of him, some rising, some falling along their shallow parabolas. And one was going to come down headfirst; at least he had not made that embarrassing miscalculation.

He landed feetfirst, throwing up a small cloud of dust. Letting his momentum pivot him forward, he waited until his body had swung through a right angle before bounding upward again.

The secret of lunar racing, he quickly discovered, was not to jump so high that you came down too steeply and lost momentum on impact. After several minutes of experimenting he found the right compromise, and settled down to a steady rhythm. How fast was he moving? There was no way of telling in this featureless terrain, but he was more than halfway to the first one-kilometer marker.

More important—he had overtaken all the others; no one else was within a hundred meters of him. Despite the "never look back" advice, he could afford the luxury of checking on the competition. He was not in the least surprised to find that there were now only three others in the race.

"Getting lonely out here," he said. "What's happened?"

This was supposed to be a private circuit, but he doubted it. The other teams and the news media would almost certainly be monitoring him.

"Goddard had a slow leak. What's your status?"

"Condition 7."

Any listeners might well guess what this meant; no matter. Seven was supposed to be a lucky number, and Singh hoped that he could keep using it until the end of the race.

"Just passing one klick," said the voice in his ear. "Elapsed time four minutes ten seconds. Number Two is fifty meters behind you, keeping his distance."

I ought to do better than that, thought Singh. Even on Earth, anyone can do a four-minute kilometer. But I'm just getting into my stride.

At the second kilometer, he had established a steady, comfortable rhythm, and covered the distance in just under four minutes. If he could keep it up—though of course that was impossible—he would reach the finishing line in about three hours. No one really knew how long it would take to run the Marathon's traditional forty-two kilometers on the Moon; guesses had ranged from a highly optimistic two hours up to ten. Singh hoped he could manage in five.

The suit seemed to be working as advertised; it did not restrict his movements unduly, and the oxygen regulator kept up with the demands made on it by his lungs. He was beginning to enjoy himself; this was not merely a race. It was something novel in human experience, opening up wholly new horizons in athletics, and perhaps much else.

Fifty minutes later, at the ten-kilometer mark, he received a message of congratulations.

"You're doing fine—and there's another dropout—Tsiolkovski's."

"What happened to her?"

"Never mind. Tell you later. But she's okay."

Singh could hazard a guess. Once, in the early days of his training, he had *almost* been sick while wearing a spacesuit. That was no trifling matter, as it could result in a very unpleasant death. He remembered the horrible clammy-cold sensation that had preceded the attack, which he had warded off by turning up the oxygen flow and the suit thermostat. He had never discovered the cause of the symptoms: it could have been nerves, or something in his last meal—a bland, high-calorie but low-residue one, since few spacesuits were equipped with full sanitary facilities.

In a deliberate attempt to divert his mind from this very unprofitable line of thought, Singh called his coach.

"I may be able to finish in a walk, if this keeps up. Three down already—and we've barely started."

"Don't get overconfident, Bob. Remember the tortoise and the hare."

"Never heard of them. But I see your point."

He saw it a little more clearly at the fifteen-kilometer mark. For some time he had been aware of an increasing stiffness in his left leg; it was getting harder to flex it when he landed, and the subsequent takeoff tended to be lopsided. He was definitely getting tired, but that was only to be expected. The suit itself still appeared to be working perfectly, so he had no real problems. It might be a good idea to stop and rest for awhile: there was nothing in the rules against it.

He came to a full stop and surveyed the scene. Little had changed, except that the peaks of Heraclides were slightly lower in the east. The retinue of moonjeeps, ambulance, and observation car still kept a respectful distance behind the racers—now down to only three. . . .

He was not surprised to see that Clavius Industries, the other lunar entry, was still in the race. What was quite unexpected was the performance the Earthworm from MIT was putting up. Robert Steel—what an odd coincidence that they had the same first name and initials—was actually ahead of Clavius. Yet he could never have had any realistic practice: did MIT's engineers know something that the locals didn't?

"You all right, Bob?" his coach asked anxiously.

"Still 7. Just taking a break. But I'm wondering about MIT. He's doing very well."

"Yes, for an Earthie. But remember what I said about not looking back. We'll keep an eye on him."

Concerned but not worried, Singh concentrated briefly on

some exercises that would have been totally impossible in a conventional suit. He even lay down in the soft regolith—the lunar topsoil, plowed by eons of meteor bombardment—and pedaled briskly for a few minutes, as if riding an invisible bicycle. Here was another first for the Moon; he hoped the spectators appreciated it.

When he got to his feet again he could not resist a quick glance backward. Clavius was a good three hundred meters behind, weaving from side to side in a manner that almost certainly indicated fatigue. Your suit designers aren't as good as mine, Singh told himself; I don't think I'll have your company for much longer.

That was certainly not true of Mister Robert from MIT. If anything, he seemed to be getting closer.

Singh decided to change his mode of locomotion, to exercise a new set of muscles and reduce the risk of cramp—another danger that his coach had warned him against. The kangaroo hop was efficient and fast, but a bounding stride was more comfortable and less tiring, simply because it was more natural.

By the twenty-kilometer mark, however, he switched back to kangaroo mode to give all his muscles an equal chance. He was also becoming thirsty, and sucked a few cc's of fruit juice from the nipple conveniently placed in his helmet.

Twenty-two kilometers to go—and now there was only one other contestant. Clavius had finally given up; in this first Lunar Marathon, there would be no bronze. It was a straight fight between Moon and Earth.

"Congratulations, Bob," chuckled his coach a few kilometers later. "You've just made exactly two thousand giant leaps for mankind. Neil Armstrong would have been proud of you."

"I don't believe you've been counting them, but it's nice to know. I'm having a small problem."

"What is it?"

"Sounds funny—but my feet are getting cold."

There was such a long silence that he repeated his complaint.

"Just checking, Bob. I'm sure it's nothing to worry about."

"I hope so."

It did indeed seem a trivial matter, but there are no trivial problems in space. For the last ten or fifteen minutes Singh had been aware of a mild discomfort; he felt that he was walking in snow, wearing shoes or boots that were failing to insulate him from the cold. And it was getting worse.

Well, there was certainly no snow on the Bay of Rainbows, though the Earthlight often gave that illusion. But here at local midnight, the regolith was much colder even than the snow of the Antarctic winter—at least a hundred degrees colder.

It should not have mattered; the regolith was a very poor conductor of heat, and the insulation on his footwear should have given him ample protection. Obviously, it was failing to do so.

An apologetic cough echoed around the inside of his helmet.

"Sorry about this, Bob. I guess those boots should have had thicker soles."

"Now you're telling me. Well, I can put up with it."

He was not so sure twenty minutes later. Discomfort was beginning to escalate to pain; his feet were starting to freeze. He had never been in a really cold climate, and this was a novel experience; he was not sure how to handle it, or when the symptoms might become dangerous. Didn't polar explorers risk losing toes—even whole limbs? Quite apart from the discomfort it would involve, Singh did not want to waste time in a regeneration ward. It took a whole week to regrow a foot. . . .

"What's wrong?" queried the anxious voice of his coach. "You seem to be in trouble."

He wasn't in trouble: he was in agony. It took all his willpower not to cry out in pain every time he hit the surface, and plowed into the deadly dirt that was sucking his life away.

"I've got to rest for a few minutes and think this over."

Singh lowered himself carefully onto the gently yielding ground, wondering if the chill would strike instantly through the upper part of his suit. But there was no sign of it, and he relaxed: he was probably safe for a few minutes, and would receive plenty of warning before the Moon tried to freeze his torso.

He raised both legs and flexed his toes. At least he could feel them, and they were obeying instructions.

Now what? The media people in the observation truck must think he was crazy, or performing some obscure religious ritual—presenting the soles of his feet to the stars. He wondered what they were telling their far-flung audiences.

Already he felt a little more comfortable; his blood circulation was winning the battle against heat-loss now that he was no longer in contact. (But was that imagination—or did he feel a slight chill in the small of his back?)

He was suddenly struck by another disquieting thought. I'm warming my feet against the night-sky—the Universe itself. And as every schoolboy knows, that's at three degrees above absolute zero. By comparison, the lunar regolith is hotter than boiling water.

So am I doing the right thing? Certainly my feet don't seem to be losing the battle against the cosmic heat-sink.

Lying almost prone on the Bay of Rainbows, holding his legs at a ridiculous angle toward the barely visible stars and the brilliant Earth, Robert Singh mulled over this little problem in physics. There were perhaps too many factors involved for an easy answer, but this one would do for a first approximation. . . .

It was a question of conduction versus radiation. The material of his space-boots was better at the first than the second. They lost his body heat faster than he could generate it when they were in physical contact with the lunar regolith. But the situation was reversed when they were radiating into the empty sky. Luckily for him.

"MIT is catching up on you, Bob. Better get moving."

Singh had to admire his persistent follower. He deserved a Silver. But damned if I'll let him win the Gold. So here we go again. Only another ten kilometers—let's say a couple of thousand hops.

The first three or four were not so bad, but then the cold began to seep through once more. Singh knew that if he stopped again, he would not be able to continue. The only thing to do was to grit his teeth and pretend that pain was merely an illusion that could be banished by an effort of will. Where had he seen a perfect example of that? He had covered another agonizing kilometer before he could locate it in his memory.

Years ago he had seen a century-old video of fire-walking, performed in some religious ceremony on Earth. A long pit had been dug, filled with red-hot embers—and the devotees had walked quite slowly and casually from one end to the other in bare feet, showing little more concern than if they were strolling on sand. Even if it proved nothing about the power of any deity, it was an astonishing demonstration of courage and self-confidence. Surely he could do as well; it was now only too easy to imagine that he was walking on fire. . . .

Fire-walking on the Moon! He could not help laughing at the concept, and for a moment the pain almost disappeared. So "mind over matter" did work—at least for a few seconds.

"Only five klicks—you're doing fine. But MIT is overtaking you—don't relax."

Relax! How Singh wished that he could. Because the biting pain in his feet had dominated all else, he had almost overlooked the increasing fatigue that was making it more and more difficult to move forward. He had abandoned jumping, and had compromised with a slow, swinging stride that would have been impressive enough on Earth, but was pitiful on the Moon.

At three kilometers he was about to give up and call for the ambulance; perhaps it was already too late to save his feet. And then, just as he felt that he was at the end of his tether, he noticed something that he would certainly have seen before had he not been concentrating all his senses on the ground immediately ahead.

The far horizon was no longer a dead straight line dividing the glowing landscape from the black night of space: he was approaching the western limits of the Bay of Rainbows, and the gently rounded peaks of Promontory Laplace were rising above the curve of the Moon. The sight—and the knowledge that his own efforts had lifted those mountains into view— gave Singh a final burst of strength.

And now nothing else in the Universe existed but the finish line. He was only a few meters from it when his tenacious opponent streaked ahead of him in an apparently effortless burst of speed.

•　•　•

WHEN ROBERT SINGH RECOVERED CONSCIOUSNESS, HE WAS LYING IN-side the ambulance, aching all over but with no pain at all.

"You're not going to do much walking for a while," he heard a voice say, light-years distant. "Worst case of frostbite I ever saw. But I've given you a local anesthetic—and you won't have to buy a new set of feet."

That was some consolation, but it hardly compensated for the bitterness of knowing that he had failed, despite all his efforts, when victory seemed so close at hand. Who was it had said: "Winning isn't the most important thing—it's the *only* thing"? He wondered if he would even bother to collect his silver medal.

"Your pulse is back to normal—how do you feel?"

"Terrible."

"Then this may cheer you up. Are you ready for a shock—a pleasant one?"

"Try me."

"You're the winner—no, don't try to get up!"

"How—what??"

"The IOC's furious, but MIT is laughing its head off. As soon as the race was over, they confessed that their Robert was really *Robot*—General Purpose Homiform Mark 9. No wonder he—it—came in first! So your performance was all the more impressive. The congratulations are pouring in. You're famous—whether you like it or not."

•   •   •

THOUGH THE FAME DID NOT LAST, THE GOLD MEDAL WAS ONE OF Robert Singh's most valued possessions for the rest of his life. Yet he did not realize what he had started until the Third Lunar Olympics, eight years later. By then the space medics had borrowed the deep-sea divers' technique of "liquid breathing," flooding the lungs with oxygen-saturated fluid.

And so the winner of the first Moon Marathon, together with most of the scattered human species, watched in awed admiration as the vacuum-proofed Karl Gregorios made his record two-minute, one-kilometer dash across the Bay of Rainbows—as naked as his Greek ancestors in the very first Olympics, three thousand years earlier.

10

A MACHINE FOR LIVING IN

AFTER HE HAD GRADUATED FROM ARRI TECH WITH SUSPICIOUSLY high marks, Astro Specialist Robert Singh had no difficulty in securing a position as assistant engineer (propulsion) on one of the regular Earth-Moon shuttles—popularly known, for some now-forgotten reason, as milk runs. This suited him admirably because, to her surprise, Freyda had now discovered that the Moon was an interesting place after all: she decided to spend a few years there, specializing in the lunar equivalent of the gold rushes that had once taken place on Earth. But what prospectors had long sought on the Moon was something much more valuable than that now-commonplace metal.

It was water—or, to be more accurate, ice. Although the eons of bombardment and occasional vulcanism that had churned up the upper few hundred meters of the Moon's surface had long ago removed all traces of water—liquid,

solid, or gaseous—there was still a hope that deep underground, near the poles, where the temperature was always far
below freezing, there might be layers of fossil ice left over
from the days when the Moon condensed out of the Solar
System's primordial debris.

Most selenologists thought this was pure fantasy, but there
had been enough tantalizing hints to keep the dream alive.
Freyda was lucky enough to be one of the team that discovered the first of the South Polar Ice Mines. Not only would
this ultimately transform the economy of the Moon, but it had
an immediate and highly beneficial impact upon the Singh-
Carroll economy. Between them, they now had enough credit
to rent a Fullerhome, and live anywhere on Earth they
pleased.

On Earth. They still expected to spend much of their lives
elsewhere, but they were eager to have a son. If he was born
on the Moon, he would never have the strength to visit the
world of his parents. A one-gee pregnancy, on the other hand,
would give him the freedom of the Solar System.

They also agreed that their home's first location should be
the Arizona desert. Though it was now becoming rather
crowded, there was still plenty of pristine geology for Freyda
to clamber over. And it was the nearest analogue to Mars,
which they were both determined to visit someday—"before
it's spoilt," as Freyda commented, only half joking.

The more difficult problem was deciding which model Fullerhome they should choose from the many varieties available.
Named after the great Twentieth-Century engineer-architect
Buckminster Fuller, and using technologies he had dreamed
of but never lived to see, they were virtually self-contained
and could sustain their occupants almost indefinitely.

Power was provided by a hundred-kilowatt sealed fusor
unit, which required topping-up with enriched water every
few years. Such a modest energy level was quite adequate for

any well-designed home, and ninety-six volts DC could elec-
trocute only the most determined suicide.

To technically minded clients who asked "Why *ninety-six
volts?*" the Fuller Consortium explained patiently that engineers were creatures of habit: only a couple of centuries ago
twelve- and twenty-four-volt systems had been standard, and
arithmetic would have been much easier if humans had twelve
fingers instead of ten.

It had required almost a century to gain general public
acceptance of the Fullerhome's most controversial feature—
the food-recycling system. Doubtless it had taken even longer,
at the beginning of the agricultural era, before hunter-gatherers had overcome their revulsion at spreading animal dung
over their future food. For thousands of years the pragmatic
Chinese had gone even further, using their own wastes to
fertilize their rice fields.

But food prejudices and taboos are among the strongest
that control human behavior, and logic is often not enough to
overcome them. Recycling excrement out in the fields, with
the help of good clean sunlight, was one thing: to do it in
one's own home with mysterious electrical devices was quite
another. For a long time the Fuller Consortium argued in
vain: "Not even God can tell the difference between one carbon atom and another." Most members of the public were
convinced that *they* could.

In the end, economics won, as is usually the case. Never
having to worry about food bills again, and having a virtually
unlimited range of menus available in the memory of the
Homebrain was a temptation few could resist. Any remaining
qualms were overcome by a transparently simple but effective
device: a small garden could be supplied, as an optional extra.
Though the recycling system could work just as well without
it, the sight of beautiful flowers turning their faces to the sun
helped to settle many queasy stomachs.

There had been only two previous owners of the Fullerhome that Freyda and Robert rented (the Consortium never sold them) and the guaranteed Mean Time to Failure of its major units was fifteen years. By then they would need another model, large enough to accommodate an energetic teenager also.

Somehow, they never did get around to asking the Brain for the usual greetings left by the earlier occupants. Both of them had their thoughts and dreams too firmly fixed upon a future, which, like all young couples, they could not believe would ever come to an end.

11
FAREWELL TO EARTH

TOBY CARROLL SINGH WAS BORN IN ARIZONA, AS HIS PARENTS HAD planned. Robert continued to serve on the Earth-Moon shuttle, rising to the position of senior engineer and even turning down a chance of going to Mars, as he did not wish to be away from his infant son for months at a time.

Freyda remained on Earth, and in fact seldom left the American Commonwealth. Though she had given up field trips, she was able to continue her researches unabated, and in considerably more comfort, via data banks and satellite imagery. It was now an old joke that geology had ceased to be a profession for husky he-men, since image-processing algorithms had replaced hammers.

Toby was three years old when his parents decided that friendly robot playmates were not enough. A dog was the obvious choice, and they had almost acquired a mutated Scottie (canine IQ guaranteed 120) when the first minitiger kittens became available. It was love at first sight.

The Bengal tiger is the most beautiful of all the big cats—and perhaps of *all* mammals. By the early Twenty-first Century it had become extinct in its natural habitat, shortly before the habitat itself had vanished. But several hundred of the magnificent creatures still led pampered lives in zoos and reservations: even if every one of these died, their DNA had of course been completely sequenced and it would be a fairly straightforward job to re-create them.

Tigrette was one by-product of such genetic engineering—to all appearances, she was a perfect example of her species, but would weigh only thirty kilograms even when full grown. Her disposition—also carefully engineered—was that of any affectionate, playful cat. Singh never tired of watching her stalking the little cleaning robots, which she obviously regarded as animals who must be investigated very cautiously, because their scent-patterns could not be found in her ancestral memories. For their part, the robots did not know what to make of her; sometimes, when she was sleeping, they mistook her for a rug and tried to vacuum-clean her, with hilarious results.

This opportunity did not often arise, because the minitiger usually slept in Toby's bed. Freyda had objected to this for hygienic reasons, until she observed how much more time the minitiger spent grooming herself than Toby devoted to his brief contacts with soap and water. Any contamination would not be in the direction she feared.

Tigrette was slightly smaller than a full-grown domestic cat when she entered the household, and quickly took it over. Robert soon complained, only half seriously, that Toby no longer noticed when his father was away in space.

Perhaps it was Tigrette's arrival that prompted another change. Freyda had always felt an attraction for the continent of her ancestors, and cherished a tattered copy of Alex Haley's *Roots* that had been in her family for generations.

"Besides," she said, "there have never been tigers in Africa. It's time there were."

On the whole, they were happy in their new location, despite occasional reminders of its hideous past—such as when Toby, digging on the beach, uncovered the skeleton of a child, still clutching a doll. For many nights thereafter he woke up screaming, and not even Tigrette's presence could comfort him.

By Toby's tenth birthday—celebrated by the arrival of three real aunts and uncles and several dozen honorary ones —both Robert and Freyda realized that the first phase of their relationship was over. Its novelty, not to mention its passion, had long since worn off; they were becoming no more than good friends who took each other's company for granted. Both of them had acquired other lovers, with a minimum of jealousy. Several times they had experimented with threesomes, and once with a foursome. Despite the best will on all sides, the results had always been comic rather than erotic.

The final break had nothing to do with any human relationships. Why, Robert Singh often wondered, did we give our hearts to friends whose life spans are so much shorter than our own?

Long ago the jungle tide would have obliterated the metal plate bearing the inscription

TIGRETTE
HERE LIE FOREVER BEAUTY, LOYALTY, STRENGTH

Though it now seemed in another lifetime, Robert Singh would never forget how Toby's boyhood had ended, as he held Tigrette in his arms while the light slowly faded from her loving eyes.

It was time to leave.

12

THE SANDS
OF
MARS

THOUGH HE HAD ALWAYS BEEN DETERMINED TO GO THERE EVENTU-
ally, Robert Singh left for Mars rather late in his life's agenda:
he was already fifty-five when, once again, Chance decided
when and how.

Tourists from Mars were rare on the Moon, and, owing to
the very effective quarantine established by its gravity, virtually unknown on the home planet. Many pretended that they
didn't really mind: everyone knew that Earth was noisy,
smelly, polluted, and horribly overcrowded—almost three *billion* people! Not to mention dangerous, with its hurricanes,
earthquakes, volcanoes . . .

Charmayne Jorgen, however, was looking wistfully Earthward in the Arri Tech observation lounge when Robert Singh
first encountered her. The twenty-meter-wide dome, a masterpiece of engineering, was so transparent that there seemed
to be nothing holding back the vacuum of space; some ner-

vous visitors could endure the experience for only a few minutes.

During his busy student days, Robert Singh had scarcely ever been there, but he was now showing one of his shipmates around his old alma mater, and this was an obligatory stop. As they walked through the three sets of automatic doors, he commented:

"If the dome blows, the outer pair closes in one second. Then the third set operates after a fifteen-second delay, to give anyone inside time to reach safety."

"Unless they're sucked out. When was it last tested?"

"Let's see—here's the certification. It's dated—ah—two months ago."

"I don't mean *that;* any dumb circuit can slam doors. Has there ever been a *real* test?"

"Like cracking the dome? Silly question. Do you know what it cost?"

At this point, the good-natured bantering ceased abruptly as the two visitors realized that they were not alone.

The silence went on and on. Finally Robert Singh's companion said:

"If you haven't lost your tongue, Bob, at least you might introduce us."

•   •   •

HE WAS STILL ON EXCELLENT TERMS WITH FREYDA, BUT THEY SAW each other less and less often now that she had moved back to Arizona and Toby had won a Moscow Conservatory scholarship—to the delighted surprise of his parents, neither of whom had ever shown the slightest musical talent. So it seemed perfectly natural that when Charmayne Jorgen returned to Mars, Robert Singh followed just as quickly as it could be arranged. With his qualifications—and the still-lingering echoes of his modest fame, which he had no scruples exploiting when necessary—this was not difficult. Soon after his fifty-sixth birthday he landed at Port Lowell. He was a New Martian—and always would be, since he had been born off-world.

"I don't mind them calling me a New Martian," he told Charmayne, "as long as they smile when they say it."

"They will, darling," she answered. "With your Earth muscles, you're a lot stronger than most people around here."

That was true, but he did not know for how long. Unless he exercised more rigorously than he suspected he would, he would soon become Mars-adapted.

Which was not without its advantages. The Martians claimed that their world, not Venus, should have been called the planet of love. Earth's one-gravity was ridiculous—if not dangerous. Weight-induced broken ribs, cramps, and interrupted blood circulation were merely some of the hazards that terrestrial lovers had to face. The Moon's one sixth gravity was a great improvement, but experts considered that it was not quite enough for good contact.

And as for the much-touted zero gee of space—after the initial novelty had worn off, it became something of a bore. One had to spend too much time worrying about rendezvous and docking problems.

The one-third gee of Mars was just about right.

•   •   •

LIKE ALL NEW IMMIGRANTS, ROBERT SINGH SPENT HIS FIRST FEW weeks doing the Martian Grand Tour—Olympus Mons, Mariner Valley, the South Polar Ice Cliffs, the Hellas Lowlands. . . . Hellas was currently popular among adventurous youngsters, who liked to show off by seeing how long they could survive without breathing gear. Atmospheric pressure was now just sufficient for such feats, though the oxygen content was still too low to sustain life. The misleadingly named "Open Air" record now stood at just over ten minutes.

Singh's initial reaction to Mars was one of slight disappointment. He had made so many virtual journeys over the Martian landscape, often at exhilarating velocities and with image enhancement, that the real thing was sometimes an anticlimax. The problem with the planet's most famous features was their sheer size—they were so enormous that they could be appreciated only from space, not when you were actually standing on them.

Olympus Mons was the best example. Martians were fond of saying that it was three times the height of any mountain on Earth—but the Himalayas or the Rockies were far more impressive because they were so much steeper. With a base six hundred kilometers across, Olympus was more like a huge blister on the face of Mars than a mountain. Ninety percent of it was nothing more than a gently sloping plain.

And Mariner Valley, except at its narrower sections, also failed to live up to the tourist promotion. It was so wide that from its center *both* walls were below the horizon: if that had not been just the sort of tactlessness that was always getting New Martians into trouble, Singh might have made disparaging comparisons with the far smaller Grand Canyon.

After a few weeks, however, he began to appreciate subtleties and beauties that explained the colonists' (that was another word he must be careful never to use) passionate devotion to their planet. And although he knew perfectly well that the land area of Mars was almost the same as Earth's, owing to the absence of oceans, he was continually surprised by its scale. Forget the fact that it was only half the diameter of Earth; it was a *big* world. . . .

And it was changing, though still very slowly. Mutated lichens and fungi were breaking down the oxidized rocks, and reversing the death-by-rust that had overtaken the planet eons ago. Perhaps the most successful invader from Earth was a modification of the "window cactus"—a tough-skinned plant that looked as if Nature had set out to design a spacesuit. Attempts to introduce it on the Moon had failed, but it was flourishing in the Martian lowlands.

Everyone on Mars had to work for a living, and though Robert Singh had made a substantial credit transfer from his healthy account on Earth, he was no exception to the rule. Nor did he wish to be: he still had decades of active life ahead of him, and wished to use it to the full—as long as he could spend as much time as possible with his new family.

That was another reason for coming to Mars; it was still an empty world, and he would be allowed two children here. His first daughter, Mirelle, was born within a year of landing; Martin came three years later. It was another five years before Captain Robert Singh felt the slightest desire to "breathe space"—or at least deep space; he was too content with his family and his work.

Of course, he made frequent trips up to Phobos and Deimos, usually in connection with his highly responsible (and well rewarded) duties as a ship surveyor for Lloyds of Earth. There was not much to do on Phobos, the inner and larger satellite, except to inspect the Space Apprentices' Training School, where he was regarded with considerable awe by the cadets. For his part, he enjoyed meeting them: it made him feel thirty—well, twenty—years younger, and also kept him in touch with the latest developments in space technology.

At one time Phobos had been regarded as an invaluable source of raw materials for space-construction projects, but Martian conservationists—perhaps feeling guilty about the steady terraforming of their own planet—had managed to prevent this. Though the tiny coal-black satellite was so inconspicuous in the night sky that few people ever noticed it, "Don't strip-mine Phobos!" had been an effective slogan.

Fortunately, the smaller and more distant Deimos was in some ways an even better alternative. Although it averaged little more than a dozen kilometers across, it could supply the local dockyards with most of the metals they needed for centuries, and no one really cared if the tiny moon slowly disappeared over the next thousand years. Moreover, its gravitational field was so feeble that only a good push was needed to launch its products on their way.

Like all busy harbors since the beginning of time, Port Deimos was an untidy mess. The first time Robert Singh ever set eyes on *Goliath* was in Deimos Yard 3, when it was undergoing a five-yearly inspection and refit. At first sight there was nothing unusual about the ship; it was no uglier than most deep-spacecraft. With an empty mass of ten thousand tons and an overall length of one hundred and fifty meters, it was not particularly large and its most important characteristic was invisible. *Goliath*'s hot fusion rocket engines, normally using hydrogen as working fluid but able to operate with water if necessary, were far more powerful than needed for a vessel of its size. Except for tests lasting only a few seconds, they had never been run at full thrust.

The next time Robert Singh saw *Goliath* she was once again at Deimos, after another uneventful five years on station. And her captain was about to retire. . . .

"Think about it, Bob," he said. "Easiest job in the Solar System. No navigation to worry about; you just sit there and admire the view. Only problem—the care and feeding of about twenty mad scientists."

It was tempting; though he had filled many responsible posts, Robert Singh had never commanded a ship, and it was about time that he did so before he retired. True, he had only just passed his sixtieth birthday, but it was amazing how quickly the decades now seemed to be slipping by.

"I'll talk it over with the family," he said. "As long as I can shuttle back to Mars a couple of times a year. . . ."

Yes—it was an attractive proposal. He would consider it carefully. . . .

Robert Singh never gave more than a few moments' thought to the purpose behind *Goliath*'s original construction. Indeed, he had almost forgotten why the ship was fitted with such a ridiculously powerful drive.

Of course, he would never have to use more than a small fraction of it; but it was nice to have it in reserve.

13
THE SARGASSO
OF
SPACE

"STAND ON THE SUN," MENDOZA HAD ONCE TOLD A CLASS OF
slightly bemused students soon after the announcement of his
Nobel Prize, "and look straight at Jupiter, three quarters of a
billion kilometers away. Then open your arms sixty degrees
on either side. . . . Do you know what you'll be pointing
at?"

He did not expect an answer, and did not pause for one.

"You won't be able to *see* anything there, but you'll be
pointing at two of the most fascinating places in the Solar
System. . . .

"In 1772 the great French mathematician Lagrange discovered that the gravitational fields of the sun and Jupiter could
combine to produce a very interesting phenomenon. Lying on
Jupiter's orbit—sixty degrees ahead, and sixty degrees behind
—are two stable points. A body placed at either will remain at

the same distance from the sun and from Jupiter, the three forming a huge equilateral triangle.

"The existence of asteroids wasn't known when Lagrange was alive, so he probably never guessed that one day there'd be a practical demonstration of his theory. It took more than a hundred years—one hundred thirty-four, to be exact—before Achilles was discovered, trailing sixty degrees behind Jupiter. A year later Patroclus was found not far away—and then Hector, but at the point sixty degrees *ahead* of Jupiter. Today we know more than ten thousand of these Trojan asteroids, so called because the first few dozen were named after the heroes of the Trojan War. Of course, *that* idea had to be given up years ago: now they simply have numbers. The last catalogue I saw had reached 11,500, and they're still coming in, though very slowly. We believe the census is now ninety-five percent complete: any remaining Trojans can't be more than a hundred meters across.

"Now I have to confess I've been lying to you. Virtually none of the Trojans are *at* the two Trojan points—they wander back and forth, and up and down, through thirty degrees or more. Saturn's largely to blame for that; its gravitational field spoils the neat sun-Jupiter pattern. So think of the Trojan asteroids as forming two huge clouds, with their centers approximately sixty degrees on either side of Jupiter. For some reason that's still unknown—anyone want a good Ph.D. thesis?—there are three times as many Trojans *ahead* of Jupiter as behind.

"Have you ever heard of the Sargasso Sea, back on old Earth? I thought not. Well, it's an area of the Atlantic—that's the ocean to the east of the CAS—in which drifting objects—weeds, abandoned ships—accumulate because of circulating currents. I like to think of the Trojan points as twin Sargassos of Space; they're the most densely populated regions of the Solar System—though you wouldn't realize it if you were actually there. If you were standing on one Trojan, you'd be very lucky if you could see another with the naked eye.

"Why are the Trojans important? I'm so glad you asked me that.

"Quite apart from their scientific interest, they're major weapons in the armory of Jove. Every so often one of them gets pulled out of place by the united fields of Saturn and Uranus and Neptune, and goes wandering sunward. And occasionally one of them crashes into us—that's how the Hellas Basin was made—or even the Earth.

"This sort of thing was happening all the time in the early days of the Solar System, when the debris left over from planet-building was still floating around. Most of it's gone now, luckily for us—but there's plenty left, not all of it in the Trojan Clouds. There are rogue asteroids that go all the way out to Neptune; any one could be a potential danger.

"Now, until this century there was nothing—absolutely nothing—that the human race could do about this danger, and most people—even if they knew about it—didn't give a damn. They felt that there were more important problems to worry about, and of course they were right.

"But a wise man takes out insurance against even very unlikely events, as long as the premium isn't too high. The SPACEGUARD survey has been running, on a very modest budget, for almost half a century. We now know that there's a high probability of at least one catastrophic impact on Earth, Moon, or Mars during the next thousand years.

"Should we just sit and wait for it? Surely not! Now that we have the technology to protect ourselves, at least we can make plans that can be put into action if—no, *when!*—there's an imminent danger. With any luck we should have several months of warning time.

"Now I've a good reason for going to Earth—that's still top secret—I want to give them a big surprise! I'm proposing a

long-range plan to deal with the problem. As a start I'm suggesting that SPACEGUARD be given an operational responsibility so that it can begin to live up to its name. I'd like to
see a couple of fast, powerful ships on permanent patrol—
and the Trojan points would be a good place to locate them.
They could do valuable research while they were there—and
they would be able to go anywhere in the Solar System at a
moment's notice.

"That's the story I'm going to tell all the Earthworms I
meet. Wish me luck."

14

THE AMATEUR

BY THE END OF THE TWENTY-FIRST CENTURY THERE WERE VERY FEW sciences in which an amateur could hope to make important discoveries—but astronomy, as it always had been, remained one of them.

True, no amateur—however affluent—could hope to match the equipment routinely used by the great observatories on Earth, the Moon, and in orbit. But the professionals specialized in narrow fields of study, and the Universe is so enormous that they could never look at more than a tiny fraction of it at one time. There was plenty left over for energetic and knowledgeable enthusiasts to explore: you did not have to own a very big telescope to find something that no one else had ever seen, if you knew how to set about it.

Dr. Angus Millar's duties as registrar at Port Lowell Medical Center were not exactly demanding; unlike terrestrial colonists, settlers on Mars had no new and exotic diseases to contend with, and most of a doctor's work involved dealing with accidents. It was true that some peculiar bone defects had turned up in the second and third generations, doubtless owing to the low gravity; but the medical establishment was confident that it would be able to deal with them before they became serious.

Thanks to his ample spare time, Dr. Millar was one of the few amateur astronomers on Mars. Over the years he had built a series of reflectors—grinding, polishing, and silvering the mirrors by techniques that thousands of devoted telescope-makers had perfected over a period of centuries.

At first he had spent much time observing the planet Earth, despite the amused comments of his friends. "Why bother?" they had asked. "It's really quite well explored—it's even supposed to harbor intelligent life-forms."

But they became silent when Millar showed them the beautiful blue crescent hanging there in space, with the smaller but identically phased Moon hovering beside it. All of history, except for the last few moments, lay there in the field of the telescope. However far it traveled out into the Universe, the human species could never wholly break its bonds to the home planet.

However, the critics had a point: Earth was not a very rewarding subject for observation. Much of it was usually covered with clouds, and when it was at its closest, only the nightside was turned toward Mars, so that all natural features were invisible. A century earlier, the "dark side" of Earth had been anything but that, as megawatts of electricity were thrown wastefully into the sky. Though a more energy-conscious society had put a stop to the worst abuses, most cities of any size could still be easily detected as glowing islands of light.

Dr. Millar wished he could have been around on Earth Date 10 November 2084 to observe that rare and beautiful phenomenon—the transit of Earth across the face of the sun. It had looked like a small, perfectly circular sunspot as it moved slowly across the solar disc, but at the midpoint of its passage a brilliant star had blazed at its center. Batteries of lasers on the dark side of Earth were greeting the Red Planet in the midnight sky that was now Mankind's second home. All of Mars had watched, and the event was still recalled in tones of reverent awe.

There was another date in the past, however, for which Dr. Millar felt a particular affinity, owing to a perfectly trivial coincidence of no interest to anyone but himself. One of the largest craters on Mars had been named after another amateur astronomer, who happened to share his birth date—two centuries earlier.

As soon as good photographs of the planet started coming back from the first space probes, finding names for all the thousands of new formations became a major problem. Some choices were obvious—famous astronomers, scientists, and explorers such as Copernicus, Kepler, Columbus, Newton, Darwin, Einstein. Next came authors who had been associated with the planet—Wells, Burroughs, Weinbaum, Heinlein, Bradbury. And then a miscellaneous list of obscure terrestrial places and individuals, some having only the most tenuous connection with Mars.

The new inhabitants of the planet were not always happy with the place names bequeathed to them, which they had to use in their everyday lives. Who or what on Earth—let alone on Mars—were Dank, Dia-Cau, Eil, Gagra, Kagul, Surt, Tiwi, Waspam, Yat?

The Revisionists were always agitating for more appropriate—and more euphonious—names and most people agreed with them. So a standing committee was set up to deal with this problem, even though it was hardly the most pressing one affecting human survival on Mars. As everybody knew that he had plenty of spare time, and was interested in astronomy, it was inevitable that Dr. Millar was co-opted.

"Why," he was asked one day, "should one of the biggest craters on Mars be named Molesworth? It's one hundred seventy-five kilometers across! Who the hell was Molesworth?"

After some research, and several expensive spacefaxes to Earth, Millar was able to answer this question. Percy B. Molesworth was an English railway engineer and amateur astronomer who made and published many drawings of Mars at the beginning of the Twentieth Century. Most of his observations were made from the equatorial island of Ceylon, where he died in 1908 at the young age of forty-one.

Dr. Millar was impressed; Molesworth must have loved Mars, and deserved his crater. The fact that they had the same birthday in the Terran calendar gave him an illogical feeling of kinship, and he would sometimes look Earthward through his own telescope to find the island where Molesworth had passed much of his short life. As the Indian Ocean was usually cloudy, he found it only once, but that was an unforgettable experience. He wondered what the young Englishman would have thought had he known that human eyes would one day look down on his home from Mars.

The doctor won his battle to save Molesworth—indeed, there was no serious opposition when he stated his case—but it changed his own attitude toward what had been merely an absorbing hobby. Perhaps he, too, could make a discovery that would carry his name down the centuries.

He was to succeed far better than he dared hope.

•   •   •

THOUGH HE HAD BEEN A BOY AT THE TIME, DR. MILLAR HAD NEVER forgotten the spectacular return of Halley's Comet in 2061; doubtless that had something to do with his next move. Many comets—including some of the most famous—had been discovered by amateurs, who had thus secured immortality by writing their names on the heavens. Back on Earth a few centuries ago, the recipe for success had been simple: a good (but not particularly large) telescope, clear skies, an intimate knowledge of the night sky, patience—and a fair amount of luck.

Dr. Millar started with several major advantages over his terrestrial precursors. He *always* had clear skies, and despite the best efforts of the terraformers, they would remain that way for the next few generations. Because of its greater distance from the sun, Mars was also a slightly better observing platform than Earth. But most important of all, the search could be largely automated. It was no longer necessary to memorize star fields, as some of the old-timers had done, so that you could instantly recognize an intruder.

Photography had long ago made that approach obsolete. It was only necessary to take two exposures, a few hours apart, and then to compare them, to see if anything had moved. Although this could be done at leisure, sitting comfortably indoors and not shivering in the cold night, it was still extremely tedious. The young Clyde Tombaugh, back in the 1930s, had scanned literally millions of star images before discovering Pluto.

The photographic approach had lasted for more than a century before being replaced by electronics. A sensitive television camera could scan the sky, store the resultant star image, then go back and look again later. In a few seconds a computer program could do what had taken Clyde Tombaugh months—ignore all the stationary objects, and "flag" anything that had moved.

It was not really as simple as that. A naive program would rediscover hundreds of known asteroids and satellites, not to mention thousands of pieces of man-made space junk. All these had to be checked against catalogues, but this, too, could be done automatically. Anything that survived this filtering process was likely to be—interesting.

•   •   •

THE AUTO-SEARCH HARDWARE AND ITS PROGRAMS WAS NOT PARticularly expensive, but like many nonessential, high-tech items, it was not available on Mars. So Dr. Millar had to wait several months before one of Earth's scientific supply companies could ship it to him—only to find, as was so often the case, that one essential component was faulty. After an acrimonious exchange of spacefaxes, the problem was sorted out. Luckily, the doctor did not have to wait for the next mail boat; when the supplier had reluctantly disgorged circuit details, the local experts were able to get the system operating.

It worked perfectly. The very next night Dr. Millar was delighted to discover Deimos, fifteen Comsats, two ferries in transit, and the incoming flight from the Moon. Of course, he had scanned only a small portion of the sky: even out around Mars space was getting crowded. No wonder he had been offered a rather good price on the equipment; it would be virtually useless beneath the clouds of space junk now orbiting Earth.

During the course of the next year, the doctor discovered two new asteroids, less than a hundred meters across, and attempted to name them Miranda and Lorna, after his wife and daughter. The Interplanetary Astronomical Union accepted the latter, but pointed out that Miranda was a famous satellite of Uranus. Dr. Millar, of course, knew this just as well as the IAU, but he thought it worth a try in the interest of domestic harmony. They finally settled for Mira; no one was likely to confuse a hundred-meter asteroid with a giant red star.

Despite several false alarms, he found nothing new for another year, and was about ready to give up, when the program reported an anomaly. It had observed an object that *seemed* to be moving—but so slowly that it could not be certain, within the limits of error. It suggested making another observation, after a longer interval of time, to settle the matter one way or the other.

Dr. Millar looked at the tiny spot of light; it could have been a faint star, but the catalogues showed nothing in this position. To his disappointment, here was no trace of the fuzzy halo that would indicate a comet. Just another damned asteroid, he thought; hardly worth bothering to go after. However, Miranda would soon give him a brand-new daughter: it would be nice to have a birthday present for her. . . .

•   •   •

IT *WAS* AN ASTEROID, JUST BEYOND THE ORBIT OF JUPITER. DR. MILLAR set the computer to calculate its approximate orbit, and was surprised to find that Myrna—as he decided to call it—came quite close to Earth. That made it slightly more interesting.

He was never able to get the name recognized. Before the IAU could approve it, additional observations had given a much more accurate orbit.

And then only one name was possible: Kali, the goddess of destruction.

•   •   •

WHEN DR. MILLAR DISCOVERED KALI, IT WAS ALREADY HEADING sunward—and Earthward—at an unprecedented velocity. Although the matter was now of somewhat academic importance, everyone wanted to know why SPACEGUARD, with all its resources, had been beaten by an amateur observer on Mars using largely home-built equipment.

The answer, as is usual in such cases, was a combination of bad luck and the well-known cussedness of inanimate objects.

Kali was extremely faint for its size, being one of the

darkest asteroids ever discovered. Obviously it belonged to the carbonaceous class: its surface was—almost literally—soot. And for the last few years the stellar background across which it had moved had been one of the most crowded parts of the Milky Way. As seen from the SPACEGUARD observatories, it had been lost in a blaze of stars.

Dr. Millar, from his viewpoint on Mars, had been lucky. He had deliberately pointed his telescope at one of the less densely packed regions of the sky—and Kali happened to be there. A few weeks earlier or later, and he would have missed it.

Needless to say, during the resulting inquiry SPACE-GUARD rechecked its terabytes of observations. When you know that something is there, it is much easier to find it.

Kali had been recorded three times, but the signal had been near the threshold of noise and so had failed to trigger the automatic search program.

Many people were thankful for the oversight; they felt that discovering Kali earlier would merely have prolonged the agony.

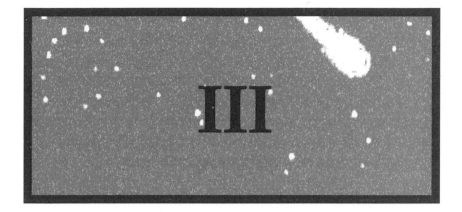

III

15

THE
PROPHET

"Isn't it time you admitted, John, that Jesus must have been an ordinary man, like Mohammed (Peace be upon him)? We know something that the writers of the Gospels didn't, though it seems perfectly obvious when you think about it—a virgin birth could produce only a female—never a male. Of course, the Holy Ghost might have contrived a second miracle. Perhaps I'm biased, but I feel that would have been—well, showing off. Even in bad taste."

—PROPHET FATIMA MAGDELENE (*SECOND DIALOGUE WITH POPE JOHN PAUL XXV,* ED. FR. MERVYN FERNANDO, SJ, 2029)

CHRISLAM WAS NOT YET OFFICIALLY A HUNDRED YEARS OLD, THOUGH its origins went back another two decades to the oil war of 1990. One of the unexpected results of that disastrous miscalculation was that large numbers of American servicemen and women had, for the first time in their lives, direct contact with Islam—and were deeply impressed. They realized that many of their prejudices, such as the popular images of mad mullahs brandishing the Koran in one hand and a submachine gun in the other, were ludicrous oversimplifications. And they were astonished to discover the advances that the Islamic world had made in astronomy and mathematics during the Dark Ages in Europe—a thousand years before the United States was born.

Delighted at this opportunity of obtaining new converts, the Saudi authorities had set up information centers at the main Desert Storm military bases to provide Islamic teaching and explanations of the Koran. By the time the Gulf War was over, some thousands of Americans had acquired a new religion. Most of them—apparently ignorant of the atrocities perpetrated upon their ancestors by the Arab slave-traders— were African-Americans, but substantial numbers were white.

Technical Sergeant Ruby Goldenberg was not merely white; she was the daughter of a rabbi and had never seen anything more exotic than Disneyland before being posted to King Faisal Base, Dhahran. Although she was well versed in both Judaism and Christianity, Islam was a new world to her; she was fascinated by its serious-minded concern for fundamental issues as well as its long-standing though now badly eroded tradition of tolerance. She particularly admired its wholehearted respect for those two prophets of different faiths—Moses and Jesus. However, with her "liberated" Western outlook, she had strong reservations about the position of women in the more conservative Muslim states.

Sergeant Goldenberg was much too busy servicing the electronics of ground-to-air missiles to become heavily involved in religious affairs until Desert Storm had blown itself out, but the seed had been planted. As soon as she returned to the

United States she used her veteran's educational entitlement to enroll in one of the few Islam-oriented colleges—a move that involved not only a fight with the Pentagon bureaucracy but a break with her own family. After only two semesters she gave a further demonstration of independence by getting herself expelled.

The facts behind this undoubtedly decisive event have never been fully established. The Prophet's hagiographers claim that she was victimized by her instructors, who were unable to answer her penetrating critiques of the Koran. Neutral historians gave a more down-to-earth explanation: she had an affair with a fellow student, and left as soon as her pregnancy was obvious.

There may be truth in both versions. The Prophet never disowned the young man who claimed to be her son, nor did she make any serious attempt to conceal later involvements with lovers of both genders. Indeed, a relaxed attitude to sexual matters, almost approaching that of Hinduism, was one of the most striking differences between Chrislam and its parent religions. It certainly contributed to its popularity: nothing could have been a greater contrast to the puritanism of Islam and the sexual pathology of Christianity, which poisoned the lives of billions and culminated in the perversion of celibacy.

After her expulsion from college, Ruby Goldenberg virtually disappeared for more than twenty years. Tibetan monasteries, Catholic orders, and a host of other claimants later advanced proofs of hospitality, none of which stood up to investigation. Nor is there any proof that she spent time on the Moon; it would have been easy to trace her in the relatively small lunar population. All that is certain is that the Prophet Fatima Magdelene appeared on the world scene in 2015.

Christianity and Islam had been accurately described as religions of the book. Chrislam, their offspring and intended successor, was based upon a technology of immeasurably greater power.

It was the first religion of the byte.

16
PARADISE CIRCUIT

EVERY AGE HAS ITS CHARACTERISTIC LANGUAGE FULL OF WORDS THAT would have been meaningless a century earlier, and many of which are forgotten a century later. Some are generated by art, sport, fashion, or politics; but most are the products of science and technology—including, of course, war.

The sailors who plied the world's oceans for millennia had a complex—and to landlubbers, incomprehensible—vocabulary of names and commands that allowed them to control the rigging on which their lives depended. When the automobile began to spread across the continents at the beginning of the Twentieth Century, dozens of strange new words came into use, and old ones were given new meanings. A Victorian hansom-cab driver would have been completely baffled by gearshift, clutch, ignition, windshield, differential, spark plug, carburetor—words his grandson would use effortlessly in everyday life. And he in his turn would be equally at a loss with radio tube, antenna, wave band, tuner, frequency. . . .

The electronic age, and particularly the advent of computers, spawned neologisms at an explosive rate. Microchip, hard disc, laser, CD Rom, VCR, tape cassette, megabyte, software—these words would have been utterly meaningless before the mid-Twentieth Century. And as the millennium approached, something still stranger—indeed paradoxical—began to appear in the vocabulary of information processing: Virtual Reality.

The results produced by the early VR systems were almost as crude as the first television displays, yet they were impressive enough to be habit-forming, even addictive. Three-D, wide-angle images could grasp the attention of the subject so completely that their jerky, cartoonlike quality was ignored. As definition and animation steadily improved, the virtual world came closer and closer to the real one, but it could always be distinguished from it as long as it was presented through such clumsy contrivances as head-mounted displays and servo-operated gloves. To make the illusion perfect, and fool the brain completely, it would be necessary to bypass the external sense organs of eyes, ears, and muscles, and to feed information directly into the neural circuits.

The concept of the "dream machine" was at least a hundred years old before developments in brain scanning and nanosurgery made it possible. The first units, like the first computers, were massive racks of equipment occupying whole rooms—and, like computers, they were miniaturized with astonishing speed. However, their application was limited as long as they had to operate through electrodes implanted in the cerebral cortex.

The real breakthrough came when—after a whole generation of medical specialists had declared it impossible—the Brainman was perfected. A memory unit storing terabytes of information was linked by a fiberoptic cable to a snugly fitting skullcap carrying literally billions of atom-size terminals, making painless contact with the skin of the cranium. The Brainman was so invaluable not only for entertainment but for education that within a single generation everyone who could afford it had acquired one—and had accepted baldness as the necessary price.

Though quite *trans*portable, the Brainman was never made truly portable, and for excellent reasons. Anyone who walked around while totally immersed in a virtual world—even in familiar home surroundings—would not survive for long.

Although the Brainman's potential for vicarious experience —especially erotic, thanks to the swiftly developing technology of hedonics—was recognized at once, its more serious applications were not neglected. Instant knowledge and skills became available through whole libraries of specialized "memory modules" or memnochips. Most appealing of all, however, was the "total diary" which allowed one to store and then relive precious moments of life—and even to re-edit them to bring them closer to the heart's desire.

Thanks to her background in electronics, the Prophet Fatima Magdelene was the first to recognize the potential of the Brainman for spreading the doctrines of Chrislam. She had, of course, precursors in the Twentieth Century televangelists who had exploited the radio waves and the communications satellites, but the technology she could deploy was infinitely more powerful. Faith had always been more a matter of emotion than intellect; and the Brainman could appeal directly to both.

Sometime during the first decade of the Twenty-first Century, Ruby Goldenberg had made an important convert—one of the extremely wealthy but now burned out (in his fifties) pioneers of the computer revolution. She gave him a new reason to live and a challenge that once again inspired his imagination; on his part, he had the resources—and even more important, the personal contacts—to meet that challenge.

It was a very straightforward project to incorporate the three Testaments of the Latter-Day Koran in electronic form, but that was merely the beginning—Version 1.0 (Public). Next came the interactive edition, intended only for those who had shown a genuine interest in the Faith and wished to proceed to the next step. However, Version 2.0 (Restricted) could be copied so easily that millions of unauthorized modules were soon circulating: which was exactly what the Prophet intended.

Version 3.0 was a different matter; it had copy protection and self-destructed after a single use. Infidels joked that it was classified "most sacred," and there was endless speculation about its contents. It was known to contain Virtual Reality programs that gave previews of the Chrislamic Paradise—but only from the outside, looking in. . . .

It was rumored—but never confirmed, despite the inevitable "exposés" of disaffected apostates—that there was a "Top Sacred" version, presumably 4.0. This was supposed to operate through advanced Brainman units, and to be "neuorologically encrypted" so that only the individual for which it was designed could receive it. Use by any unauthorized person would result in permanent mental damage—perhaps even insanity.

Whatever technological aids Chrislam employed, the time was ripe for a new religion, embodying the best elements of two ancient ones (with more than a touch of an even older one, Buddhism). Yet the Prophet might never have succeeded without two other factors, wholly beyond her control.

The first was the so-called "Cold Fusion" revolution, which brought about the sudden end of the Fossil Fuel Age and destroyed the economic base of the Muslim world for almost a generation—until Israeli chemists rebuilt it with the slogan "Oil for Food—Not for Fire!"

The second was the steady decline in the moral and intellectual status of Christianity, which had started (though few realized it for centuries) on October 31, 1517, when Martin Luther nailed his Ninety-five Theses to the door of All Saints Church. The process was continued by Copernicus, Galileo, Darwin, Freud, and culminated in the notorious "Dead Sea-gate" scandal, when the final release of the long-hidden Scrolls revealed that the Jesus of the Gospels was based on three (perhaps four) separate individuals.

But the coup de grace came from the Vatican itself.

17
ENCYCLICAL

"Exactly four centuries ago, in the year 1632, my predecessor, Pope Urban the Eighth, made an appalling blunder. He allowed his friend Galileo to be condemned for teaching what we now know to be a fundamental truth, that the Earth goes around the sun. Though the Church apologized to Galileo in 1992, that dreadful mistake gave a blow to its moral standing from which it never fully recovered.

"Now, alas, the time has come to admit an even more tragic error. Through its stubborn opposition to family planning by artificial means, the Church has wrecked billions of lives—and, ironically, been largely responsible for promoting the sin of abortion among those too poor to support the children they were forced to bring into the world.

"This policy has brought our species to the verge of

ruin. Gross overpopulation has stripped Planet Earth of its resources and polluted the entire global environment. By the end of the Twentieth Century everyone realized that—yet nothing was done. Oh, there were conferences and resolutions without number—but little effective action.

"Now a long-hoped-for—and long-feared!—scientific breakthrough threatens to turn a crisis into a catastrophe. Though the whole world applauded when Professors Salman and Bernstein received the Nobel Prize for Medicine last December, how many have stopped to consider the social impact of their work? At my request, the Pontifical Academy of Science has just done so. Its conclusions are unanimous—and inescapable.

"The discovery of superoxide enzymes that can retard the aging process by protecting the body's DNA has been called a triumph as great as the breaking of the genetic code. *Now, it appears, the span of healthy* and active *human life can be extended by at least fifty years— perhaps much more! We are also told that the treatment will be relatively inexpensive. So whether we like it or not, the future will be a world full of vigorous centenarians.*

"My Academy informs me that the SOE treatment will also lengthen the period of human fertility by as much as thirty years. The implications of this are shattering—especially in view of past dismal failures to limit births by appeals for abstinence and the use of so-called 'natural' methods. . . .

"For several weeks now, the experts of the World Health Organization have been networking all its members. The goal is to establish the often-discussed but never achieved, except in times of war and plague, zero

population growth as quickly—and humanely—as possible. Even that may not be sufficient; we may need negative *population growth. For the next few generations the one-child family may have to be the norm.*

"The Church is wise enough not to fight against the inevitable, especially in this radically changed situation. I will shortly be issuing an encyclical that will contain guidance on these matters. It has been drawn up, I might add, after full consultation with my colleagues the Dalai Lama, the Archbishop of Canterbury, the Chief Rabbi, Imam Mahommud, and the Prophet Fatima Magdelene. They are in complete agreement with me.

"Many of you, I know, will find it hard—even agonizing—to accept that practices the Church once stigmatized as sins must now become duties. *On one fundamental point, however, there has been no change in doctrine. Once a fetus is viable, its life is sacred.*

"Abortion remains a crime, and will always be so. But now there is no longer any excuse—or any need— for it.

"My blessings to you all, on whatever world you may be listening."

—JOHN PAUL XXV, EASTER 2032: EARTH-MOON-MARS
NEWS NETWORK

18
EXCALIBUR

IT WAS THE LARGEST SCIENTIFIC EXPERIMENT EVER MADE, BECAUSE IT embraced the entire Solar System.

EXCALIBUR's origins went back to the bizarre—indeed, now hardly believable—days of the almost forgotten "cold war," when two superpowers had confronted each other with nuclear weapons that could destroy the very fabric of civilization, and perhaps even threaten the survival of Mankind as a biological species.

On one side was the entity calling itself the Union of Soviet Socialist Republics—which, as later historians were fond of pointing out, might have been a soviet (whatever *that* meant) but was certainly neither a union, nor socialist, nor a republic. On the other side was the United States of America, named with considerably greater accuracy.

By the last quarter of the Twentieth Century, the two opponents possessed thousands of long-range rockets, each capable of carrying a warhead that could destroy a city. Understandably, attempts were made to find counterweapons that could prevent such missiles from reaching their targets. Prior to the discovery of force fields—more than a hundred years later—no complete defense was possible, even in theory. Nevertheless, frantic efforts were made to design antimissile missiles and laser-equipped orbiting fortresses that could provide at least partial protection.

Looking back on those times, it is difficult to decide whether the scientists who advanced some of these schemes were cynically exploiting the genuine fears of naive politicians, or sincerely believed that their ideas could be turned into practical reality. Those who did not live in the aptly named "century of sorrows" should not judge them too harshly.

Undoubtedly the craziest of all the counterweapons proposed was the X-ray laser. It was theorized that the enormous energy produced by the explosion of a nuclear bomb could be converted into highly directional beams of X-rays so powerful that they could destroy enemy missiles thousands of kilometers away. The EXCALIBUR device (understandably, full details were never published) would have resembled a sea urchin, spines pointing in all directions, with a nuclear bomb at its center. Each spine would, in the microseconds before it evaporated, generate a laser beam—every one aimed at a different missile.

It needs little imagination to see the limitations of such a "single shot" weapon, especially against an enemy who refused to cooperate by launching his missiles in convenient bunches. Nevertheless, the basic theory behind the bomb-powered laser was sound, though the practical difficulties of creating it had been grossly underestimated. In fact, the whole project was abandoned after scores of millions of dollars had been wasted upon it.

Yet not entirely wasted. Almost a century later the concept was revived, again as a defense against missiles, but this time those created by Nature, not by Man.

The Twenty-first-Century EXCALIBUR was designed to produce radio waves, not X-rays, and they were not aimed at specific targets, but the entire celestial sphere. The gigaton bomb—the most powerful ever made, and, most people hoped, the most powerful that ever *would* be made—was exploded in Earth orbit but on the other side of the sun. That would provide the maximum protection from the tremendous electromagnetic pulse that might otherwise wreck communications and burn out electronic equipment all over the planet.

When the bomb exploded, a thin shell of microwaves—only a few meters thick—expanded across the Solar System at the speed of light. Within minutes, detectors stationed all around the orbit of the Earth started to receive echoes from the sun, Mercury, Venus, the Moon: but no one was interested in these.

For the next two hours, before the radio explosion had swept past Saturn, hundreds of thousands of echoes, becoming fainter and fainter, poured into EXCALIBUR's data banks. All known satellites, asteroids, and comets were easily detected, and when the analysis was complete, every object more than a meter in diameter inside the orbit of Jupiter had been located. Cataloguing them all, and computing their future movements, would occupy SPACEGUARD's computers for years.

The first "quick looks," however, were reassuring. There was nothing that endangered Earth within EXCALIBUR's range, and humanity relaxed. There were even suggestions that SPACEGUARD should be canceled.

When, many years later, Dr. Angus Millar discovered Kali with his homemade telescope, there was a general outcry to find why the asteroid had been missed. The answer was simple: Kali had then been at the far point of its orbit, beyond the range of even a nuclear-powered radar. EXCALIBUR would certainly have detected it had it been close enough to represent an immediate danger.

But long before that happened, EXCALIBUR had produced an awesome and wholly unexpected result. It had not merely detected a danger: many believed that it had created one, and resurrected an ancient fear.

19

THE UNEXPECTED ANSWER

SETI—THE SEARCH FOR EXTRA-TERRESTRIAL INTELLIGENCE—HAD been pursued with ever more sensitive equipment, and over a steadily increasing band of frequencies, for more than a century. There had been many false alarms, and the radio-astronomers had recorded a few "possibles" that might have been the genuine article, and not merely random fragments of cosmic noise. Unfortunately, the samples captured had all been too short for even the most ingenious computer analysis to prove that they were of intelligent origin.

All this changed abruptly in 2085. One of the old-time SETI enthusiasts had once said: "When there *is* a signal, we'll know for sure it's the real thing—it won't be a feeble hiss, almost buried in the noise." She was right.

The signal was picked up loud and clear during a routine survey by one of the smaller radio telescopes on lunar Farside —still a fairly quiet place despite the local communications traffic. And there could be no doubt of its extra-terrestrial origin. The telescope that received it was pointing directly at Sirius, the most brilliant star in the entire sky.

That was the first surprise: Sirius was some fifty times more brilliant than the sun, and had always seemed a poor candidate for life-bearing planets. The astronomers were still arguing about this when they—and the whole world—received a much bigger shock.

Though, in retrospect, the fact was blindingly obvious, it was almost twenty-four hours before someone pointed out an interesting coincidence.

Sirius was 8.6 light-years away, and Project EXCALIBUR had taken place seventeen years and three months ago. There had just been time for radio waves to travel to Sirius and back. Whoever—or whatever—had received the electromagnetic explosion had wasted no time in returning the call.

As if to clinch matters, the carrier wave from Sirius was on exactly the same frequency as the EXCALIBUR pulse—5400 megahertz. However, there was one major disappointment.

Contrary to all expectation, that 5400 MHz wave was completely unmodulated: there was no trace of a signal.

It was pure noise.

20

THE
REBORN

Few religions survive the death of their founder unscathed. So it was with Chrislam, despite Fatima Magdelene's efforts at designating a successor.

The first disagreements occurred when her son, Morris Goldenberg, materialized out of nowhere and attempted to claim his inheritance. He was first denounced as a fraudulent pretender, but when he demanded—and obtained—DNA testing, the Movement had to abandon this line of defense.

He next made the pilgrimage to Mecca, and though he was kept at a safe distance from the Kaaba, he thereafter insisted on calling himself Al Haj. How sincere he was in this—or indeed anything else—was hotly disputed. About his mother's sincerity there was never any serious doubt, but after his death most people decided that Al Haj Morris Goldenberg was nothing more than a charming and plausible adventurer, making the most of the opportunity Fate had given him. Iron-ically, he was one of the last known victims of the AIDS virus —a fact from which many discordant conclusions were drawn.

As far as outsiders were concerned, most of the matters of doctrinal dispute that Morris promoted appeared trivial: were prayers at dawn and sunset the minimum requirement; were pilgrimages to Bethlehem and Mecca of equal merit; could the Ramadan fast be cut to a week; was it necessary to give tithe to the "poor," now that Society as a whole recognized its responsibilities in this matter; how to reconcile Jesus' order to "drink wine in remembrance of me" with Muslim aversions to alcohol . . . and so on. . . .

However, after Morris's death, the disagreements between the various sects were patched up, and for several decades Chrislam showed a fairly united face to the world. At its peak it claimed over a hundred million adherents, and was the fourth most popular religion on Earth, though it made little headway on the Moon and Mars.

The major schism was triggered, very unexpectedly, by the "Voice of Sirius." An esoteric subsect, much influenced by Sufi doctrine, claimed to have interpreted the enigmatic signal from space by the use of advanced information processing techniques.

All earlier attempts had failed completely; the signal—if it was that—appeared to be unmodulated noise. Why the Siri-ans should bother to transmit pure noise was a puzzle that had spawned countless theories. The most popular one was that, like high-security messages sent in some encryption systems, it merely *looked* like noise. It could be an intelligence test, which only the Reborn had passed—if their claims were to be believed.

Yet noise of obviously artificial origin *did* convey one unmistakable message: "We are here." Perhaps the Sirians were waiting for an acknowledgment—the "electronic handshake" required by many communications devices—before they started transmitting intelligence.

The Chrislamic zealots—the "Reborn" as they were later to call themselves—had a much more ingenious answer, though not an original one. In the early days of communications theory, it had been pointed out that "pure noise" could be considered not as meaningless garbage, but as *the combined total of all possible messages.* The Reborn had a neat analogy: imagine that all the poets, philosophers, and prophets of mankind were talking *simultaneously.* The result would be a totally indecipherable torrent of sound—yet it would contain the sum total of human wisdom.

So it was with the message from Sirius. It was nothing less than the Voice of God; and only the Faithful could understand it—with the help of elaborate decrypting equipment and abstruse algorithms. When they were asked exactly what God was saying, the Reborn replied, "We will tell you at the right time."

The rest of the world laughed, of course—though there were some apprehensive grumbles when the Reborn built a kilometer-wide dish on the far side of the Moon in an attempt to start a dialogue with God—or whatever was at the other end of the circuit. None of the official space organizations had yet made such a move, because they had been unable to agree on a suitable answer. Indeed, many thought it would be best for the human race to remain silent—or simply to broadcast Bach.

Meanwhile, the Reborn, confident of their special relationship, beamed prayers and homage toward Sirius. They even claimed that because God created Einstein and not the other way around, they would not be limited by the velocity of light: their conversation would not be handicapped by seventeen-year time lags.

The detection of Kali had, for the Reborn, nothing less than the force of a revelation. Now they knew their destiny—and prepared to live up to their name.

For at least a century, few educated people had believed in Resurrection, and the Prophet Fatima Magdelene had wisely avoided the issue. Now, said the Reborn as the world was coming to an end, it was time to take the idea seriously. They could guarantee survival—at a price, of course.

Millions were already planning to emigrate to the Moon or Mars, but both destinations were already setting up quotas to prevent their limited resources from being overwhelmed. In any event, only a few percent of the human race would be able to take this escape route.

The Reborn offered something far more ambitious: not merely safety, but immortality.

They announced that they had attained one of Virtual Reality's long-sought goals: they could record a complete human being—all the memories of a lifetime, and the current map of the body that had experienced them—in a modest ten to the fourteenth bits of storage space. However, the playback—the literal Resurrection—would still require decades of research. Even if there was any point in doing so, it could not possibly be completed before Kali arrived.

No problem: the Reborn had already received God's assurance. All true believers could beam themselves toward Sirius, via the transmitter on Farside. Heaven was waiting for them at the other end.

This was the point at which most people's lingering doubts about the Reborns' sanity evaporated. Despite their undoubted technological sophistication, they were obviously as crazy as all the other Millennialists who, with monotonous regularity, had promised to save their particular disciples when the world came to an end next Tuesday.

From now on, the Reborn could be regarded as a rather sick joke; their antics were of no concern to a planet that had more serious matters to worry about.

It was an understandable mistake—and a disastrous one.

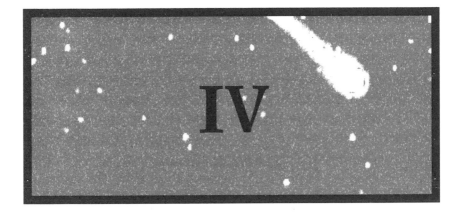

21

VIGIL

DEIMOS DOCKS CLAIMED TO BUILD THEM BY THE KILOMETER, AND let the customer saw off the length he needed. Certainly most of their products had a basic family likeness, and *Goliath* was no exception.

Its backbone was a single triangular spar, one hundred and fifty meters long and five meters across each side. It would have looked incredibly flimsy to any engineer born before the Twentieth Century, but the nanotechnology that had built it up literally carbon atom by carbon atom had given it a strength fifty times greater than the finest steel.

Along this synthetic diamond spine were fixed the various modules—most of them readily interchangeable—that comprised *Goliath*. By far the largest items were the spherical hydrogen tanks ranged along the three sides of the spar, like peas on the *outside* of a pod. In comparison, the command, service, and residential modules at one end, and the power and propulsion units at the other, looked like afterthoughts.

When he had been assigned to command *Goliath,* Robert Singh had looked forward to a peaceful—if possible, even boring—few years of space duty before he retired on Mars. Although he was only seventy, he was definitely slowing down. Being stationed here at the T1 Trojan Point, sixty degrees ahead of Jupiter, should be almost a holiday. All that he had to do was to keep his astronomer and physicist passengers happy while they conducted their endless experiments.

For *Goliath* was classified as a research vessel, and had been funded accordingly by the Planetary Science Budget. So was *Hercules,* a billion and a quarter kilometers away at the T2 point. Together with the sun and Jupiter, the two ships defined an enormous diamond, which never changed its shape but revolved around the sun once in every Jovian year of 4333 Earth-days.

As the ships were linked by laser beams whose length was known with an accuracy of better than one centimeter, it was an ideal arrangement for many types of scientific work. Ripples in space-time caused by colliding black holes—feats of cosmic engineering by super-civilizations—and who knew what else—might be detected by the arrays of instruments aboard *Goliath* and *Hercules.* And as receivers on the two ships could be linked together to form a radio telescope effectively more than a billion kilometers across, they had already been able to map remote regions of the Universe with unprecedented accuracy.

Nor had the researchers aboard the Trojan Twins neglected the immediate neighborhood, where distances were measured in mere millions of kilometers. They had observed hundreds of the asteroids caught in this vast gravitational trap, and had made short excursions to visit many of the nearer ones. In a few years, more had been learned about the composition of these minor bodies than in the three centuries since they were first discovered.

The uneventful routine, broken only by changes of personnel and regular returns to Deimos for inspection and updating of equipment, had now lasted more than thirty years, and few people remembered the purpose for which *Goliath* and *Hercules* had been originally built. Even their crews seldom stopped to think that they were on sentry duty, like the watchers who had patrolled the windy walls of Troy three thousand years before. But they were waiting for an enemy that Homer could never have imagined.

22
ROUTINE

THOUGH CAPTAIN SINGH'S CURRENT ASSIGNMENT, EQUIDISTANT from the sun and Jupiter, had been called the loneliest job in the Solar System, he seldom felt lonely. He often contrasted his situation with that of the great navigators of the past, such as Cook and the unfairly maligned Bligh. They had been cut off from all communication with their home base and their families for months—sometimes years—and had been forced to live in crowded, unhygienic quarters in close contact with a handful of fellow officers and a larger number of ill-educated and frequently mutinous seamen. Even apart from such external dangers as storms, hidden shoals, enemy action, and hostile natives, shipboard life in the old days must have been a close approximation to Hell.

It was true that there was not much more living space aboard *Goliath* than there had been on Cook's thirty-meter-long *Endeavour*—but the absence of gravity meant that it could be used far more effectively. And, of course, the amenities available to crew and passengers were incomparably superior. For entertainment, they had immediate access to everything that human art and culture had produced—up to a few minutes ago. The time lag to Earth was almost the only hardship they had to endure.

Every month there would be a fast shuttle from Mars or the Moon, bringing new faces and taking personnel home for vacation. The eagerly awaited arrival of the "Mail Boat" with items that could not be sent over radio or optical links was the only break in a now-well-established routine.

Not that shipboard life was by any means free from problems—technical and psychological, serious and trivial . . .

•   •   •

"PROFESSOR JAMIESON?"

"Yes, skipper."

"David has just drawn my attention to your exercise record. It seems that you have missed your last two sessions on the treadmill."

"Er . . . there must be some mistake."

"Undoubtedly. But whose? I'll put you through to David."

"Well, perhaps I did miss one—I've been very busy analyzing those samples they brought back from Achilles. I'll make up for it tomorrow."

"Be sure you do, Bill. I know it's boring, but unless you crank up to half a gee when your schedule tells you to, you'll never be able to walk on Mars again—let alone Earth. Captain out."

•   •   •

"MESSAGE FROM FREYDA, CAPTAIN. TOBY'S GIVING A CONCERT AT THE Smithsonian on the fifteenth—she says it will be quite an occasion. They've got hold of Brahms's original concert grand: Toby's playing one of his own compositions, and Rachmaninoff's Paganini variations. Would you like complete coverage, or just the audio?"

"I'll never have time to enjoy either—but I don't want to hurt Toby's feelings. Send my best wishes—and order the whole memnochip."

• • •

"DR. JAWORSKI?"

"Yes, Captain."

"There's an extraordinary smell coming from your lab. Several people have complained to me. The air filters don't seem to be able to handle it."

"Smell? Strange, I hadn't noticed anything. But I'll look into it immediately."

• • •

"CAPTAIN, THERE WAS A MESSAGE FROM CHARMAYNE WHILE YOU were sleeping. Not urgent, but your Martian citizenship will lapse in ten days unless you renew. Current transmission time to Mars is twenty-two minutes."

"Thanks, David. I can't deal with it now. Remind me this time tomorrow."

• • •

"CAPTAIN SINGH, RESEARCH SHIP *GOLIATH* TO SOLAR NEWS NETWORK. I received your report a couple of days ago but didn't take it seriously: I'd no idea those lunatics were still around. No, we have *not* encountered any alien spacecraft. Be assured we'll let you know when we do."

• • •

"SONNY?"

"Here, Captain."

"Congratulations on the table decorations last night. But my soap dispenser's run out again. Can I have a refill—pine scent this time—I'm sick of lavender."

•   •   •

BY GENERAL CONSENSUS, SONNY WAS THE SECOND MOST IMPORTANT man on board; some considered him *more* important than the captain.

His official status as ship's steward barely hinted at Sonny Gilbert's role aboard *Goliath*. He was Mister Fixit par excellence, able to cope equally well with human and technical problems—at least on the general housekeeping level. The crankiest of cleaning robots started to behave when he was in the vicinity, and lovesick young scientists of all genders were more likely to confide in him than in the SHIPDOC-PSYCH program. (Rumors had reached Captain Singh that Sonny had a remarkable collection of sex aids, real and virtual; but there were some things that a wise commander preferred not to know.)

The fact that, by any standard of measurement, Sonny had the lowest intelligence quotient of anyone aboard ship was completely unimportant; his efficiency, good nature, and sheer kindness were all that mattered. When a famous visiting cosmologist, in a fit of pique, called him a moron, Captain Singh had given the man a tongue-lashing and told him to apologize. When he refused to do so, he was sent home by the next shuttle, despite vigorous protests from Earth.

Though this was an exceptional case, there was always a certain tension between *Goliath*'s crew and the scientific passengers. It was usually quite good-natured, and took the form of wisecracks and, sometimes, practical jokes. But when there were unusual challenges, everyone cooperated wholeheartedly, quite regardless of their official duties.

Since David kept an unsleeping eye on all *Goliath*'s operating systems, no round-the-clock watch was necessary. During the "day," both the A and B crews were awake, though only one was on duty; then the whole ship closed down for eight hours. Should an emergency occur, David could react more swiftly than any human: indeed, if there was any situation that even he could not handle, it would probably be kinder to leave both crews sleeping for the few remaining seconds of their lives.

Ship's day began at 06.00 universal time, but because the galley was too small to accommodate everyone, the crew that was first on duty had priority at the 06.30 breakfast. B crew ate at 07.00, and the scientist passengers had to wait until 07.30. However, as snacks were available at any time from the automat, no one ever had to suffer the pangs of hunger.

Promptly at 08.00, Captain Singh gave a summary of the day's program and reported any important news. Then the A crew dispersed for duty, the scientists went to their labs and consoles, and the B crew disappeared into their small but luxurious cubicles to catch up on the overnight news videocasts, plug into the ship's information and entertainment systems, do some studying, and otherwise occupy themselves until the switchover at 14.00 hours.

That was the nominal time-line, but it was subject to frequent perturbations, both planned and unplanned. The most interesting of these were occasional excursions to passing asteroids.

It was not true, as a blasé astronomer had remarked, "When you've seen one asteroid, you've seen them all." (He was an expert on colliding galaxies, so his ignorance of such minor details could be excused.) In fact, asteroids came in almost as many varieties as sizes—from the thousand-kilometer Ceres down to nameless rocks the size of a small apartment building.

Most of them were, in fact, nothing but rock, of kinds

perfectly familiar on Earth or the Moon—basalts and granites, the high-grade building materials specified by the original Architect of the Alps and the Himalayas.

Others were largely metal: iron, cobalt, and rarer elements, including gold and platinum. Some quite small asteroids would have been worth trillions of dollars in the days before commercial transmutation had made gold slightly cheaper than much more useful metals like copper or lead.

The asteroids that were of the greatest interest to science, however, were the ones containing large quantities of ice and carbon compounds. Some were extinct comets—or comets that were yet to be born when the shifting tides of gravity nudged them toward the generative fires of the sun.

The carbonaceous asteroids still held many mysteries. There were signs—though the evidence was still hotly disputed—that some of them had once been part of a much larger body, perhaps even a world big enough, and warm enough, to possess oceans. And if that were the case, why not life itself? Several paleontologists had damaged their reputations by claiming to have discovered fossils in asteroids, and although most of their colleagues pooh-poohed the idea, the jury was still out.

Whenever an interesting asteroid came within range, *Goliath*'s scientists were likely to become polarized into two groups: though they never actually came to blows, seating arrangements at meals were liable to undergo subtle changes. The astrogeologists wanted to move the ship—and all their laboratory equipment—to make a rendezvous with the target so that they could examine it at leisure. The cosmologists fought against this tooth and nail; their carefully measured baselines would be altered, and all their interferometry ruined —just for a few miserable hunks of rock.

They had a point, and the geologists would eventually compromise with more or less good grace. The smaller passing asteroids could be visited by robot probes, able to pick up samples and carry out most basic surveying operations. This was better than nothing, but if the asteroid was more than a million kilometers away, the *Goliath*-probe–*Goliath* transmission lag became intolerable. "How would *you* like to swing a hammer," one geologist had complained, "and have to wait for a minute before you knew you'd missed?"

So for really important passersby such as major Trojans like Patroclus or Achilles, the ship's launch would be made available for the eager scientists. Not much larger than a family automobile, it could provide basic life support for pilot and three passengers for up to a week, allow them to do a fairly detailed examination of the virgin worldlet, and bring back a few hundred kilograms of well-documented samples.

On the average, Captain Singh had to arrange such expeditions every two or three months. He welcomed them, as they gave some variety to shipboard life. And it was noticeable that even the scientists who expressed the most disdain for such rock-grubbing watched the incoming videos as eagerly as anyone else.

They gave various excuses:

"Helps give me some of the feeling my great-great-grandparents must have had when they watched Armstrong and Aldrin first step on the Moon."

"Gets at least three rockhounds out of the way for a week. More room at mealtimes too."

"Don't quote me on this, Captain, but if there ever have been any visitors to the Solar System, this is where they may have left some of their garbage. Or even a message for us to find, when we're advanced enough to understand it."

Sometimes, as he watched his colleagues floating over weird miniature landscapes that no one had ever before visited—or probably ever would again—Singh had felt an impulse to get away from the ship and enjoy the freedom of space. He could probably find an excuse to do so: his first officer would be only too happy to take over for a while. But he would be a supercargo—even a nuisance—in the cramped quarters of the launch, and could not justify such an indulgence.

Yet it seemed a pity to spend several years at the center of this veritable Sargasso Sea of drifting worlds and never set foot on any of them.

One day he would certainly have to do something about it.

23

ALARM

IT WAS AS IF THE SENTRIES ON THE WALLS OF TROY HAD CAUGHT THE first glitter of sunlight on distant spears. Instantly, everything was changed.

And yet the danger was still more than a year away. Formidable though it was, there was no sense of immediate crisis: indeed, there was still hope that the initial hasty observations might be in error. Perhaps the new asteroid would miss Earth after all, as so many myriads of others had done in past ages.

David had awakened Singh with the news, at 05.30 UT; it was the first time he had ever broken the commander's sleep.

"Sorry about this, Captain. But it's classed absolute priority —I've never seen one before."

Nor had Singh, and he was instantly wide awake. As he read the spacefax, and looked at the orbit of Earth and asteroid it displayed, he felt as if a cold hand had fastened itself upon his heart. He hoped there could be some mistake: but even from that first moment he never doubted the worst.

And then, paradoxically, a sense of elation swept over him. This was what *Goliath* had been built for, decades ago.

And this was his moment of destiny. On the Bay of Rainbows, when he was little more than a boy, he had met one challenge—and overcome it. Now he was faced with an immeasurably greater one.

This was why he had been born.

•   •   •

NEVER GIVE ANYONE BAD NEWS ON AN EMPTY STOMACH. CAPTAIN Singh waited until all aboard had eaten breakfast, then relayed the spacefax from Earth—and the follow-up that had arrived an hour later.

"All programs, all research projects, are of course canceled. The science staff will return to Mars on the next shuttle, while we prepare *Goliath* for what will certainly be the most important mission that it—that *any* ship—has ever been given.

"Details are now being worked out, and may be changed later. As I'm sure you know, plans for a mass-driver that could deflect an asteroid of reasonable size were drawn up years ago: it was even given a name—ATLAS. As soon as all mission parameters are known, those plans will be finalized, and Deimos Docks will go into high-speed construction. Luckily all the necessary components are standard items—propellant tanks, thrusters, control systems, and the framework to hold them together. So the nanoassemblers can build ATLAS in a few days.

"Then it will have to be mated with *Goliath*—so we have to get to Deimos as quickly as possible. That will give some of us a chance to see our families on Mars: there's an old Earth proverb that says 'It's an ill wind that blows nobody any good.' . . .

"We'll take on just enough propellant to carry the empty ATLAS to Jupiter, and refuel at the Europa orbital tank farm. And then the *real* mission will begin—the rendezvous with the asteroid. By then it will be only seven months from Earth impact—if it *is* going to impact.

"We'll have to survey the asteroid, locate a suitable foundation, install ATLAS, check all systems—and start up the drive. Of course, its effect on a body massing a billion tons will be almost too small to measure. But a deflection of a few centimeters, if it can be applied before the asteroid passes Mars orbit, will be sufficient to make it miss Earth by hundreds of kilometers. . . ."

Singh paused, feeling a little embarrassed. All this was elementary stuff for the crew, but it would be unfamiliar to the geologists and astrochemists. He seriously doubted if they could tell him Kepler's Three Laws, much less compute an orbit.

"I'm no good at making inspirational speeches, and I don't think one is necessary. You all know what we have to do, and there's no time to waste. Even a few days lost now could make all the difference between a harmless flyby and the end of History—at least on Earth.

"One other thing. Names are very important—look at all the Trojans around us. We've just received the official designation from the IAU. Some scholar has been going through the Hindu mythology, and has come across the goddess of death and destruction.

"Her name is Kali."

24

SHORE
LEAVE

"What were the Martians *really* like, Daddy?"

Robert Singh looked fondly at his daughter—officially six years old, although the planet on which she lived had made only five circuits of the sun since she was born. No child could be expected to wait 687 days between birthdays, so this was one relic of the Earth calendar that had been retained. When it was finally abandoned, Mars would have severed yet another link with the Mother World.

"I knew you were going to ask me that," he answered. "So I've looked it up. Listen . . .

" 'Those who have never seen a living Martian can scarcely imagine the strange horror of its appearance. The peculiar V-shaped mouth with its pointed upper lip, the absence of brow ridges, the absence of a chin beneath the wedgelike lower lip, the incessant quivering of this mouth, the Gorgon—' "

"What's a Gorgon?"

" '—the Gorgon groups of tentacles—' "

"Ugh!"

" '—above all, the extraordinary intensity of the immense eyes—were at once vital, intense, inhuman, crippled, and monstrous. There was something fungoid in the oily brown skin, something in the clumsy deliberation of the tedious movements unspeakably nasty.' Well, Mirelle—now you know."

"What are *you* reading? Oh—the DisneyMars guide! When can we go?"

"That depends on how well a certain young lady does her homework."

"Not fair, Daddy! I haven't had time since you've been back!"

Singh felt a brief spasm of guilt. He had tended to monopolize his small daughter and her baby brother whenever he could escape from the ATLAS assembly and checkout on Deimos Docks. His hopes of private visits when he got down to Mars had been instantly dashed when he saw the media persons waiting for him at Port Lowell: he had not realized that he was the second most famous person on the planet.

The most famous, of course, was Dr. Millar, whose detection of Kali had changed—and perhaps would change—more lives than any event in human history. Though they had been involved in half a dozen electronic encounters, the two men had not yet met in person. Singh had avoided such a confrontation: they had nothing new to say to each other, and it was obvious that the amateur astronomer had been unable to cope with his unexpected celebrity. He had become arrogant and condescending, and always referred to Kali as "my asteroid." Well, sooner or later his fellow Martians would cut him down to size; they were very good at that.

• • •

DISNEYMARS WAS TINY COMPARED TO ITS FAMOUS TERRESTRIAL FORE-
bears, but once you were inside, there was no way of telling
that. By means of dioramas and holographic projections, it
showed Mars as men had once believed or dreamed it might
be—and as one day they hoped it would be. Although some
critics complained that a Brainman session could create exactly the same experience, that was simply untrue. One only
had to watch a Marschild stroking a piece of genuine Earth-
rock to appreciate the difference.

Martin was much too young to enjoy the excursion, and
was left in the safe care of the latest model Dorcas home
robot. Even Mirelle was not really old enough to understand
everything that she was seeing, but her parents knew that she
would never forget it. She squealed with fearful delight when
H. G. Wells's tentacled horrors emerged from their cylinders,
and watched in awe as their monstrous tripods stalked
through the deserted streets of a strange, alien city—Victorian
London.

And she loved the beautiful Dejah Thoris, Princess of He-
lium, especially when she said sweetly, "Welcome to Bar-
soom, Mirelle." John Carter, however, had been all but
eliminated from the scenario: such bloodthirsty characters
were definitely not the sort of immigrant the Martian chamber of commerce wished to encourage. Swords, indeed! Why,
if they weren't handled with great care, pieces of metal fash-
ioned with such criminal irresponsibility might cause serious
injuries to bystanders. . . .

Mirelle was also fascinated by the strange beasts that Burroughs had scattered so lavishly over the Martian landscape.
However, she was puzzled about one piece of exobiology,
which Edgar Rice had passed over rather lightly.

"Mother," she said. "Was *I* hatched from an egg?"

Charmayne laughed.

"Yes and no," she answered. "But it certainly wasn't like

the one that Dejah laid. I'll ask Library to explain the difference when we get home."

"And did they really have machines that could make air so that people could breathe outside?"

"No—but old Burroughs had the right idea. That's exactly what we're trying to do—you'll see when we've gone through the Bradbury section."

• • •

. . . AND OUT OF THE HILLS CAME A STRANGE THING.

It was a machine like a jade-green insect, a praying mantis, delicately rushing through the cold air, indistinct, countless green diamonds winking over its body, and red jewels that glittered with multifaceted eyes. Its six legs fell upon the ancient highway with the sound of a sparse rain which dwindled away, and from the back of the machine a Martian with melted gold for eyes looked down at Tomas as if he were looking into a well. . . .

• • •

MIRELLE WAS FASCINATED YET PUZZLED BY THE NIGHT MEETING OF Earthman and Martian, each a phantom to the other; one day she would understand that it was a fleeting encounter between two ages, across an abyss of time. She loved the graceful sandships gliding over the deserts, the flame-birds glowing on the cool sands, the golden spiders throwing out films of web, the boats drifting like bronze flowers along the wide-green canals. And she wept when the crystal cities crumbled before the invaders from Earth.

"From The Mars That Never Was—To The Mars That Will Be," said the sign at the entrance to the last gallery. Captain Singh could not help smiling at that "will," typically Martian in its self-confidence. On tired old Earth the verb would have been "may."

The final exhibit was almost old-fashioned in its simplicity, and none the less effective. They sat in near darkness behind a picture window, looking down upon a sea of mist, while the distant sun came up behind them.

"Mariner Valley—the Labyrinth of Night, as it is today," said a soft voice above a background of gentle music.

The mist dissolved beneath the rising sun; it was no more than the thinnest of vapors. And there was the vast expanse of canyons and cliffs of the mightiest valley in the Solar System, sharp and clear out to the horizon, with none of the softening by distance that gave a sense of perspective to similar views in the far smaller Grand Canyon of Western America.

It was austerely beautiful, with its reds and ochres and crimsons, not so much hostile to life as utterly indifferent to it. The eye looked in vain for the slightest hint of blue or green.

The sun dashed swiftly across the sky, the shadows flowed like tides of ink over the canyon floors. Night fell; the stars flashed out briefly, and were banished by another dawn.

Nothing had changed—or had it? Was the far horizon no longer so sharp-edged?

Another "day," and there could be no doubt. The harsh contours of the terrain were becoming softened; distant cliffs and scars were no longer so sharply defined. Mars was changing. . . .

The days—weeks—months—perhaps they were really decades—flickered past. And now the changes were dramatic.

The faint salmon hue of the sky had given way to a pale blue, and at last real clouds were forming, not tenuous mists that vanished with the dawn. And down on the floor of the canyon, patches of green were spreading where once there had been only barren rock. There were no trees as yet, but lichens and mosses were preparing the way.

Suddenly, magically, there were pools of water—lying calm

and unruffled in the sun, not flashing instantly into vapor as they would on Mars today. As the vision of the future unfolded, the pools became lakes, and merged into a river. Trees sprouted abruptly along its banks: to Robert Singh's earth-conditioned eyes, their trunks appeared so slender that he could not believe they were more than a dozen meters tall. In reality—if one could call this reality!—they would probably out-top the tallest redwood: a hundred meters at a minimum, in this low gravity.

Now the viewpoint changed; they were flying eastward along Mariner Valley, out through the Chasm of the Dawn, and southward to the great plain of Hellas, the lowlands of Mars. It was land no longer.

As he looked down upon the dream ocean of a future age, a flood of memories poured into Robert Singh's mind, with such overwhelming power that for a moment he almost lost control of himself. The Hellas Ocean vanished; he was back on Earth, walking along that palm-fringed African beach with little Toby, with Tigrette padding close behind them. Did that *really* happen to him, once upon a time, or was it a false past, the borrowed memory of another person?

Of course he had no real doubts, but the flashback was so vivid that it left an afterimage burning in his mind. However, the sense of sadness quickly gave way to a mood of wistful contentment. He had no regrets—Freyda and Toby were both well and happy (it was high time he called them again!) with extended families to look after them. He was sorry, though, that Mirelle and Martin would never experience the joy of having nonhuman friends like Tigrette. Pets of any kind were a luxury that Mars could not yet afford.

The voyage into the future ended with a glimpse of the planet Mars from space—how many centuries or millennia hence?—its poles no longer crowned with caps of frozen carbon dioxide as sunlight beamed down from hundred-kilometer-wide orbiting mirrors ended their age-long winter. The image faded, to be replaced by the words SPRING, 2500. I wonder—I hope so, though I shall never know, thought Robert Singh as they walked out in silence. Even Mirelle seemed unusually subdued, as if trying to disentangle the real from the imaginary in what she had seen.

As they were walking through the airlock to the pressurized Marscar that had brought them from the hotel, the exhibition produced one final surprise. There was a roll of distant thunder—a sound that only Robert Singh had ever heard in reality —and Mirelle gave a little shriek as a shower of fine droplets fell upon them from an overhead sprinkler.

"The last rain on Mars was three billion years ago—and it brought no life to the lands on which it fell.

"Next time, it will be different. Good-bye, and thank you for coming."

•   •   •

ROBERT SINGH WOKE IN THE SMALLER HOURS OF HIS LAST NIGHT before takeoff, and lay in the darkness, trying to recall the highlights of his visit. Some of them—including the tender moments of a few hours earlier—he had recorded for future playback: they would sustain him in the long months ahead.

The change in his breathing rhythm must have disturbed Charmayne: she rolled toward him and rested her arm on his chest. Not for the first time, Singh smiled as he recalled how uncomfortable this gesture could be on the home planet.

For several minutes neither spoke. Then Charmayne said sleepily: "You remember that Bradbury story we looked up— the one where those barbarians from Earth used the beautiful crystal cities for target practice?"

"Of course. 'And the Moon be still as bright.' I couldn't help noticing that he set it in 2001. A little too optimistic, wasn't he?"

"Well, at least he did live to see men get here! But I couldn't help thinking, after we left DisneyMars—aren't we behaving in exactly the same way, destroying what we've found?"

"Never thought I'd hear a true Marschild talk like that. But we're not just destroying. We're creating . . . my God . . ."

"What's the matter?"

"That's just reminded me. Kali. She's not only the goddess of destruction. She also creates a new world out of the wreckage of the old."

A long silence. Then:

"That's exactly what the Reborn keep telling us. Did you know that they've set up a mission right here in Port Lowell?"

"Well, they're harmless lunatics. I don't suppose they'll bother anyone. Happy dreams, darling. And next time we go to DisneyMars we'll take Martin—I promise."

25

EUROPA
STATION

ROBERT SINGH HAD LITTLE TO DO ON THE FAST RUN FROM DEI-
mos/Mars to Europa/Jupiter, except to study the constantly
changing contingency plans SPACEGUARD kept beaming to
him—and to get to know the new members of his crew.

Torin Fletcher, a senior engineer from Deimos Docks,
would supervise the refueling operations when the *Goliath/*
TITAN combination reached the tank farm orbiting Europa.
The tens of thousands of tons of hydrogen to be pumped
aboard would be in the form of slush—a mixture of liquid
and solid denser than the pure liquid and thus requiring less
storage space. Even so, the total volume was more than twice
that of the ill-fated *Hindenburg,* whose fiery doom had closed
the brief age of lighter-than-air transportation—at least on
Earth. Small freight-carrying airships were often used on
Mars, and had proved valuable for research in the upper atmosphere of Venus.

Fletcher was an airship enthusiast, and did his best to convert Singh.

"When we *really* start the exploration of Jupiter," he said, "and don't just drop probes into it—that's when the airship will come into its own again. Of course, since the atmosphere is mostly H_2, it will have to be a hot-hydrogen airship—no problem! Imagine—riding around the Great Red Spot!"

"No thank you," Singh had replied. "Not at ten Mars gravity."

"Earthies could take it lying down. Or on water beds."

"But why bother? There's no solid surface—nowhere to land—robots can do everything we want without risking humans."

"That's just the sort of argument people made when the Space Age started. Now look where we are! Men and women will go to Jupiter because—er, because it's there. But if you don't like Jupiter—how about Saturn? Almost the same gravity as Earth—and just think of the view! Cruising in high latitudes, where you can see the rings—one day that will be a major tourist attraction."

"Cheaper to plug into a Brainman. All the fun and none of the risk."

Fletcher laughed as Singh quoted the famous slogan.

"You don't believe that, of course."

He was right, but Singh had no intention of admitting it. The element of risk was what distinguished Reality from its imitations, however perfect. And the willingness to take risks —indeed, to welcome them, if they were reasonable—was what gave zest to life and made it worthwhile.

Another of the Europa-bound passengers was involved with a technology that seemed even more out of place than aeronautics—that of deep-diving submersibles. In all the Solar System, Europa was the only world apart from Earth that possessed oceans, sealed beneath a crust of ice that protected them from space. The heat produced by Jupiter's immense gravitational tides—the same forces that triggered the volcanoes of neighboring Io—kept the global ocean from freezing.

Where there was liquid water, there was hope of life. Dr. Rani Wijeratne had spent twenty years exploring the Europan abyss, both in person and by means of robot probes. Though she had found nothing, she was not discouraged.

"I'm sure it's there," she said. "I only hope I can find it before some Earth-based microbes crawl out of our garbage and take over."

Dr. Wijeratne was also quite optimistic about the prospects for life much farther from the sun—in the great cloud of comets far beyond Neptune.

"There's all the water and carbon and nitrogen and other chemicals out there," she was fond of saying. "*Millions* of times as much as on the planets. And there must be radioactivity—which means heat, and a rapid mutation rate. Conditions may be ideal for the origin of life, deep down inside comets."

It seemed a pity that the doctor would be disembarking at Europa, and not continuing on to Kali. Her good-natured but no-holds-barred debates with Sir Colin Draker, FRS, had provided the other passengers with a great deal of entertainment. The famous astrogeologist was the only scientist still aboard from *Goliath*'s original complement, being sufficiently eminent to overrule any orders to bring him home.

"I know more about asteroids than any living man," he argued with unchallengeable accuracy. "And Kali is the most important asteroid in history. I want to get my hands on it—as my one-hundredth birthday present to myself. And for the sake of science, of course."

As for the cometary life-forms suggested by Dr. Wijeratne, he had no doubts.

"Nonsense! Hoyle and Wickremasinghe suggested that over a century ago, but no one ever took it seriously."

"Then it's time they did. And since asteroids—some of them, anyway—are dead comets, have you ever looked for fossils? It might be worth doing."

"Frankly, Rani, I can think of much better ways of spending my time."

"You geologists! Sometimes I think you're all fossils yourselves! Remember how you laughed at poor Wegener and his theory of continental drift—and made him your patron saint when he was safely dead?"

And so forth—all the way to Europa.

•   •   •

EUROPA, THE SMALLEST OF JUPITER'S FOUR GALILEAN SATELLITES, WAS the only world in the Solar System that could be mistaken for Earth—if you were close enough. As Captain Singh looked down on the endless expanse of ice floes beneath him, it was easy to imagine that he was really orbiting the home planet.

That illusion vanished quickly when he turned his eyes toward Jupiter. Racing through its phases every three and a half days, the giant world dominated the sky, even when it had dwindled to a vanishingly thin crescent. For then that arc of light cradled a huge black disk twenty times the diameter of the Moon in Earth's sky—blotting out the stars and presently eclipsing the distant sun. And the night side of Jupiter was seldom completely dark; thunderstorms larger than terrestrial continents flickered back and forth, like an exchange of nuclear weapons—and with equal energy. Rings of auroral light usually draped the poles, and geysers of phosphorescence welled up from the planet's unexplored—perhaps forever unexplorable—depths.

And when it was near full, the planet was even more impressive. Then the intricate loops and curlicues of the cloud belts, eternally marching parallel to the Equator, could be seen in their multicolored glory. Along them moved pale, oval islands—like thousand-kilometer-wide amoebae; sometimes they appeared to thrust so purposefully through the cloud-scape around them that it was easy to believe they were enor-mous living creatures. More than one fanciful astro-epic had been based on just this hypothesis.

But the show-stealer was the Great Red Spot. Though it had waxed and waned over the centuries, sometimes disap-pearing almost completely, it was now more prominent than it had ever been since Cassini had discovered it in 1665. As Jupiter's dizzying ten-hour rotation swept it across the face of the planet, it looked as if a giant bloodshot eye were staring malevolently out into space.

It was no wonder that workers on Europa had the shortest tour of duty, and the highest rate of mental breakdown, of any planet-based staff. Matters had improved somewhat when facilities had been moved to the center of Farside, where Ju piter was perpetually hidden. Yet even here the psychologists reported that some patients believed that unblinking, Cyclo-pean eye was watching them through three thousand kilome-ters of solid rock. . . .

Watching them, perhaps, as they stole Europa's treasure. The satellite was the only major source of water—and hence hydrogen—within the orbit of Saturn. Although there were even greater amounts in the comet clouds far beyond Pluto, it was not yet economical to mine them. One day, perhaps . . . meanwhile Europa supplied most of the propellant for the commerce of the Solar System.

Moreover, Europan hydrogen was superior to that from Earth. Thanks to eons of bombardment from the radiation fields around Jupiter, it contained a much higher percentage of the heavier isotope deuterium. With only a little more en-richment it supplied the optimum mixture needed to power a fusion drive. Occasionally—not often—Nature cooperated with Mankind.

• • •

ALREADY IT WAS DIFFICULT TO REMEMBER LIFE BEFORE KALI. THE moment of peril was still months away, but almost every thought and action was focused upon it. And to think, Robert Singh sometimes reminded himself ironically, that I took this job because I wanted an undemanding assignment before I retired with the rank of full captain!

It was not often that he had time for such introspection, for the once-regular ship's routine had now been superseded by what his first officer had called "planned crises." And yet, in view of the complexity of Operation ATLAS, everything had gone with reasonable smoothness; there had been no major holdups, and the program was only two days behind what had once seemed to be an impossible schedule.

Once *Goliath*/ATLAS had been established in parking orbit, the lengthy process of filling their tanks with two hundred thousand tons of hydrogen-deuterium slush, at thirteen degrees above absolute zero, began in earnest. The Europan electrolysis plants could produce this amount in a week, but getting it up to orbit was another matter. By bad luck, two of Europa's tankers were undergoing major repairs, which could not be handled locally. They had been towed back to Deimos. . . .

And so, even if everything went smoothly, it would take almost a month to fill the cavernous tanks. During that time, Kali would come a hundred million kilometers closer to Earth.

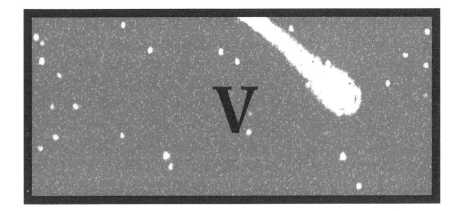

26
MASS DRIVER

VERY LITTLE OF THE ORIGINAL *GOLIATH* WAS NOW VISIBLE: THE whole of one side was concealed beneath the tanks and propulsion modules of ATLAS, a compact mass of plumbing almost two hundred meters long. Most of the remainder of the ship was also hidden by its own additional tankage. We won't have much of a view, Singh told himself, until we've dropped off some of our empties. Or much acceleration either, despite the engine upgrades, with all that extra mass.

It was difficult to believe that the future of humanity might well depend on this ungainly collection of hardware. It had been designed and assembled with one single objective in mind—to land a powerful mass driver on Kali as quickly as possible. *Goliath* was merely the delivery van, the interplanetary space-truck: ATLAS was the all-important cargo, which had to reach its destination on time, and in good condition.

Achieving this objective involved an extraordinary number

of trade-offs. Although it was essential to reach Kali with minimum delay, speed could be bought only at the expense of payload. If *Goliath* burned up too much hydrogen getting to Kali, there might not be enough left to divert the asteroid from its baleful trajectory, and the whole effort would have been in vain.

To shorten mission time without using propellant, some thought had been given to the classic "gravity boost" used by the first spacecraft to explore the outer Solar System. *Goliath* could dive in toward Jupiter and rob the giant planet of some of its momentum as it skimmed past. However, the plan had been reluctantly abandoned because of its risks; there was too much junk orbiting around Jupiter. The tenuous rings extended right down to the limits of the atmosphere, and even the smallest fragment could puncture the lightly constructed hydrogen tanks. It would be the ultimate irony if a tiny Jovian micro-moon frustrated the mission.

Unlike a liftoff from a planetary surface, there was nothing in the least dramatic about the start of an orbital transfer. There was, of course, no sound, and not even a visible indication of the awesome energies involved. The plasma jet driving *Goliath* was much too hot to emit the feeble radiations that the human eye can detect; it wrote its signature across the stars in the far ultraviolet. To the spectators watching from the Europa satellite complex, the only indication that *Goliath* had started to move was the small cloud of debris it left behind—fragments of thermal shielding, discarded packing material, pieces of string and tape—all the junk left over on a major construction project by even the most careful workers. It was not the grandest of beginnings, for so noble an enterprise: but *Goliath* and its ATLAS payload were on their way, carrying the hopes and fears of all mankind.

A day later, accelerating at a tenth of a gravity, *Goliath* lumbered past the second largest satellite, battered Callisto. But it was almost a week before it finally escaped from Jovian territory, crossing the wildly erratic orbits of the tiny outermost twins Pasiphaë and Sinope. By then it was moving so swiftly that not even the sun could call it back; it would leave the Solar System completely, if it was unable to check its speed again, and begin an endless journey among the stars.

But no spaceship commander could have hoped for a more uneventful voyage. *Goliath* and ATLAS made their rendezvous with Kali twelve seconds ahead of schedule.

•   •   •

"I'VE VISITED DOZENS OF ASTEROIDS," SAID SIR COLIN DRAKER TO HIS unseen audience half a billion kilometers sunward, "and even now, there's no way I can judge their size, merely by looking at them. I know *exactly* how big Kali is, but I could easily fool myself into thinking I could hold it between my outstretched arms.

"The problem is, there's absolutely no sense of scale— nothing to give any clue to the eye. As you'll see, it's covered with shallow impact craters right down to the limit of vision. That big one, left center, is actually about fifty meters across —but it looks exactly like the little ones all around it—the smallest you can see are a few centimeters across.

"Will you zoom in, David? Thanks—now, we're getting closer—but there's no real difference in the picture. The mini-craters we're seeing now look just like their big brothers —stop the zoom there, David—even if we used a magnifying glass, the image would look much the same—shallow craters of every possible size—right down to ones made by dust particles.

"Now pull back to show the whole of Kali again—thanks. You'll see that there's virtually no color, at least to the human eye. It's almost black—you might guess it was a lump of coal, and you wouldn't be far wrong—the outer layers are ninety percent carbon.

"Inside, though, it's different—iron, nickel, silicates, various ices—water, methane, carbon dioxide. It's obviously had a very complicated history, and in fact I'm almost certain it's an aggregate of two bodies of quite different composition that collided fairly gently and then stuck together.

"You may have noticed that some new craters have come into view while I've been talking. Kali's day is quite short—three hours twenty-five minutes. And the fact that it's rotating makes our job even trickier. . . .

"Can we have the other side, David? Center on Grid Reference K5—that's it. . . .

"Notice the change of scenery—if you can call it that. Those grooves must have been caused by another collision—this time quite a violent one. Kali must have been in a busy part of the Solar System, ten billion years ago. See that valley top right—we've christened it the Grand Canyon. It's all of ten meters deep, but if you didn't know the scale, you easily could imagine you were in Colorado. . . .

"So—we have a battered little world—shaped like a dumbbell, or a peanut—with a mass of two billion tons. And by bad luck, it's moving in a retrograde orbit—that is, in the opposite direction to all the planets. Nothing very unusual about that—Halley does just the same—but it means that it will collide with the Earth head-on—the worst possible case, of course. So we've *got* to divert it. If we don't, then not only our civilization, but even our species, may be wiped off the face of the planet.

"The ATLAS mass driver has now been detached from *Goliath*—pan to ATLAS please, David—and we're now engaged in the delicate job of installing it on Kali. Fortunately, the asteroid's gravity is so feeble—about one ten-thousandth of Earth's—that ATLAS weighs only a few tons. Don't let that fool you though. It still has all its mass—*and its momentum.* So it has to be moved very, very slowly and carefully. . . . Believe it or not, the main tools for the job are old-fashioned winches and pulleys, anchored on Kali.

"In a few hours, ATLAS will be ready to start firing. Of course, its effect on Kali will be almost too small to measure —a fraction of a microgravity. I believe some media person said it would be like a mouse pushing an elephant: true enough. But ATLAS can keep pushing for days, and we have to move Kali only a few centimeters, out here around Jupiter, for it to miss Earth by thousands of kilometers.

"And even a hundred would be as good as a light-year."

27
DRESS REHEARSAL

A BALD SIKH! HOW WOULD MY HIRSUTE ANCESTORS, BACK THERE IN India, have reacted to such an apostate? And if they knew that I'd had my scalp permanently depilated—well, I'd be lucky to escape alive. . . .

This thought invariably flashed through Robert Singh's mind when he lowered the tightly fitting skullcap over his head, adjusted the restraining straps, and checked that the eye pads were excluding all light. Then he sat in total darkness and silence, waiting for the automatic sequencer to take over.

First there was the faintest of sounds, so low-pitched that he could almost hear the separate vibrations. Still at the limit of detectability, it climbed upward octave by octave until it vanished at the edge of hearing. Indeed, *beyond* that, for though Singh had never bothered to check, he was quite sure that the mechanism of his ears could never respond to the frequencies that were now flowing directly into his brain.

Silence returned, and he waited for the far more complex vision calibration sequence to begin.

First there was pure color: he might have been floating at the center of a perfectly featureless sphere, its inner surface painted the deepest red. There was not the slightest trace of pattern or structure, and the eyes ached in the attempt to find some. No—that was not quite correct. The eyes did not come into the circuit at all.

Red—orange—yellow—green—the familiar colors of the rainbow, but in laser-sharp purity. Still no image of any kind —only an unbroken chromatic field.

At last, images began to appear. First an open grid, which filled up rapidly with reticulations that became finer and finer, until they could no longer be resolved. This was replaced by a sequence of geometric shapes—rotating, expanding, shrinking, morphing into each other. Though he had lost all sense of time, the whole calibration program had lasted less than a minute. When a soundless "white out" engulfed him like an Antarctic blizzard, he knew that the scanning process was complete, and that the Brainman's monitoring system had satisfied itself that his neural circuits were properly matched to receive its outputs.

Sometimes, though very rarely, an "error message" would flash across his field of consciousness, and he would have to repeat the whole sequence. That usually cleared the problem; if it did not, Singh knew better than to try again. Once, when he had needed to acquire some skills in a hurry, he had operated the manual override in an attempt to bypass the electronic roadblock. His reward had been a nightmare display of images, always just beyond his ability to grasp properly—like the phosphenes that result from pressure on the eyeballs, but far more brilliant. By the time he had hit the cut-out, he had acquired a splitting headache—and it could have been much worse. Irreversible "zombification" by malfunctioning Brain-men was no longer as common as in the early days of the device, but it still happened.

This time there was no error message or other warning signal. All circuits were clear. He was ready to receive.

Though some remote corner of his mind knew that he was really aboard *Goliath,* it did not appear the least incongruous to Captain Singh to be looking down upon his ship as it floated alongside Kali. It also seemed quite logical—even if it was the bizarre logic of a dream—that ATLAS was already installed on the asteroid, even though he "knew" that it was really still attached to *Goliath.*

The details of the simulation were so perfect that he could see the bare patches of rock on Kali where the jets of the space-sled had blown away the dust of ages. That was real enough; but the image of ATLAS and its cluster of fuel tanks still belonged to the future—hopefully, only a few days away. With David's assistance, all the engineering problems of positioning and anchoring the mass-driver had been solved, and there was no reason to suppose that there would be any difficulty in turning theory into practice.

"Ready to begin run," said David. "What viewpoint would you like?"

"North pole of Ecliptic. Ten A.U. distant. Show all orbits."

"*All?* There are 54,372 bodies in that field of view." The pause while David checked his catalogue was barely perceptible.

"Sorry. I mean all major planets. And any bodies that come within a thousand kilometers of Kali. Correction—make that a hundred kilometers."

Kali and ATLAS vanished. Singh was looking down upon the Solar System from above, with the orbits of Saturn, Jupiter, Mars, Earth, Venus, and Mercury visible as thin, glowing lines. The positions of the planets themselves were indicated by tiny but recognizable icons—Saturn with its rings, Jupiter with its belts, Mars with a tiny polar cap, Earth one vast ocean, Venus a featureless white crescent, Mercury a pock-marked disk.

And Kali was a skull. That had been David's own idea, and no one had ever discussed it with him. Presumably he had looked up the entry in the encyclopedia—and seen one of the statues of the Hindu goddess of destruction wearing her sinister necklace.

"Center on Kali-Earth axis—zoom in—check!"

Now Singh's consciousness was filled by that fateful conic section—the ellipse of doom that connected the present positions of Earth and Kali.

"Time compression?"

"Ten to fifth."

At that rate, every second would represent a day: Kali would reach Earth in a matter of minutes, not months.

"Starting run."

The planets began to move—Mercury speeding around its innermost track, and even lumbering Saturn creeping snail-like along its outer orbit.

Kali started its fall sunward, still moving under gravity alone. But numbers were flickering somewhere in Singh's field of consciousness, so swiftly that they blurred together. Suddenly they collapsed to zero, and at the same moment David said, "Ignition!"

Strange, Singh thought briefly, how some words remained in use long after they had lost their original context. "Ignition" dated back at least a century, to the era of chemical rockets. There was no way that the jet that powered ATLAS —or any other deep-space vessel—could burn. It was pure hydrogen—and even had there been any oxygen present, it would have been far too hot for the low-temperature phenomenon of mere combustion. Any water molecules would have been instantly ripped back to their component atoms.

More figures appeared, some constant, others changing very slowly. Most prominently displayed was the acceleration produced by the ATLAS jet in this phantom world—mere microgravities, upon a mass the size of Kali. And here were the vital deltas, the barely measurable changes now being made to the asteroid's velocity and position.

The days flickered past; the numbers steadily increased: Mercury had moved halfway around the sun, but Kali still showed no visible sign of deviation from its natural orbit. Only the increasing deltas proved that it was stirring sluggishly from its ancient path.

"Zoom five times," Singh ordered as Kali passed Mars. The outer planets vanished as the image expanded; but the effect of ATLAS's days of continuous thrusting was still undetectable.

"Burnout," said David abruptly. (Yet another word from the infancy of astronautics!) The figures that had recorded thrust and acceleration dropped instantly to zero. Kali was once more being whirled around the sun by gravity alone.

"Zoom ten. Reduce time compression to one thousand."

Now only Earth, Moon, and Kali occupied Singh's field of consciousness. On this expanded scale, the asteroid seemed to be moving not along an ellipse, but an almost straight line —and it was a line that did *not* point toward Earth.

Singh knew better than to take any hope from that. Kali had yet to pass the Moon and—like a treacherous friend betraying her old companion—she would give Kali's orbit its last murderous twist.

Now, in this final stage of the encounter, each second represented three minutes of real time. Kali's path was bending visibly in the Moon's gravitational field—bending toward

Earth. But the effect of ATLAS's efforts, though they had ceased "weeks" earlier, was also apparent. The simulation displayed two orbits—the original one, and the one produced by human intervention.

"Zoom ten. Time compression one hundred."

Now one second equaled almost two minutes, and Earth filled Singh's field of consciousness. But the tiny skull icon had remained the same size: on this scale, Kali was still too small to show a visible disk.

The virtual Earth looked incredibly real, heartbreakingly beautiful; impossible to believe it was merely a construct of superbly organized megabytes. Down there—if only in David's memory!—was the glistening white cap of the Antarctic, the continent of Australia, the New Zealand islands, the coast of China. But dominating all was the deep blue of the Pacific; only twenty generations ago it had been as great a challenge to Mankind as were the gulfs of space today.

"Zoom ten. Keep tracking Kali."

The blue curve of horizon was misty with atmosphere, merging imperceptibly into utter blackness. Kali was still dropping toward it, drawn downward and also accelerated by the Earth's gravitational field—almost as if the planet were abetting its own suicide.

"Closest approach in one minute."

Singh focused his attention on the numbers still flickering at the edge of vision. The message they carried was more precise, though less dramatic, than that given by the simulated image. The all-important one—Kali's distance from the Earth's surface—was still decreasing.

But the *rate of decrease* was itself decreasing. It was taking longer and longer for Kali to cover each new kilometer Earthward.

And then the figure stabilized: 523 . . . 523 . . . 522

. . . 522 . . . 522 . . . 523 . . . 523 . . . 524 . . . 524 . . .
525 . . .

Singh allowed himself the luxury of breath. Kali had made
its closest approach, and was drawing away.

ATLAS could do the job. Now it only remained to match
the real world with the virtual one.

28
BIRTHDAY PARTY

"I NEVER EXPECTED," SAID SIR COLIN, "TO SPEND MY HUNDREDTH birthday outside the orbit of Mars. In fact, when *I* was born, only about one man in ten could hope to reach that age. And one woman in five—which always seemed unfair to me."

(Good-natured booing from the four ladies of the crew; groans from the males. A smug "Nature knows best" from ship's physician Dr. Elizabeth Warden.)

"But here I am, in reasonably good shape, and I'd like to thank you all for your good wishes. And especially Sonny, for that marvelous vintage we've just drunk—Chateau Whatever-itwas, 2005!"

"It was *1905,* Prof—not 2005. And you should thank the kitchen programs, not me."

"Well, you're the only person who knows what's in them. We'd starve to death if you forget what buttons to press."

• • •

HUNDRED-YEAR-OLD GEOLOGISTS COULD NOT BE EXPECTED TO KIT themselves up properly, so Singh and Fletcher double-checked Draker's spacesuit before they accompanied him out of the airlock. Movement in the immediate vicinity of *Goliath* had been greatly simplified by a network of ropes, supported on meter-high rods driven into Kali's friable outer crust: the ship now looked like a spider in the center of a web.

The three men moved carefully hand-over-hand to a small space-sled, dwarfed by the spherical propellant tanks that had been lined up for later connection to ATLAS. "Looks as if some lunatic has built an oil refinery on an asteroid" had been the prof's comment when he saw what Fletcher's human-plus-robot workers had achieved in such an amazingly short time.

Torin Fletcher, used to working on Deimos, was the only man who could really handle a space-sled in the even feebler gravity of Kali. "You've got to be careful," he had warned would-be jockeys. "A snail with arthritis could reach escape velocity here. We don't want to waste time and reaction mass hauling you back if you decide to head for Alpha Centauri."

With barely perceptible puffs of gas he lifted the sled off the surface of the asteroid and started the leisurely circum-navigation of the world, while Draker eagerly scanned the regions of Kali he had never seen with his unaided eyes. Until now he had been forced to rely on specimens brought back by crew members. And although remote examination via mobile cameras was invaluable, there was no substitute for hands-on experience, aided by skillful hammer blows. Draker had complained that he could never get more than a few meters away from *Goliath,* because Captain Singh refused to run risks with his most celebrated passenger, and could spare no one to look after him outside the ship. (As if I *needed* looking after!) But a one-hundredth birthday overruled such objections, and the scientist was like a small boy on his first holiday away from home.

The sled was gliding over the surface of Kali at comfortable walking speed—assuming that a man *could* walk on this microworld. Sir Colin kept scanning like an ancient search radar from horizon to horizon (sometimes all of fifty meters distant) occasionally muttering to himself. After less than five minutes they had reached the antipodes: *Goliath* and ATLAS were both hidden by the bulk of Kali when Draker asked, "Can we stop here? I'd like to get off."

"Of course. But we'll attach a line, in case we have to reel you back."

The geologist snorted in disgust, but submitted to the indignity. Then he gently eased himself off the now-motionless sled, and relaxed in free-fall.

It was not easy to tell that he was indeed falling in this minuscule gravity; it was almost two minutes before he crashed into Kali, from an altitude of a whole meter, moving at a velocity barely perceptible to the naked eye. . . .

Colin Draker had stood on many asteroids. Sometimes, as on giants like Ceres, it was easy to tell that the force of gravity was dragging you down, even if feebly. Here it took a considerable act of imagination; the slightest movement, and Kali would lose its grip.

Yet he was, finally and indisputably, standing on the most famous—or infamous—asteroid in the whole of history. Even with his scientific knowledge it was hard for Draker to accept the fact that this tiny, erratically curved fragment of cosmic debris represented a greater threat to humanity than all the warheads stockpiled in the Age of Nuclear Madness.

Kali's swift rotation was taking them into night, and as their eyes adapted, they watched the stars come out around them—in exactly the patterns that Earth-based observers would see, for they were still so close to the home planet that the outer universe appeared completely unchanged. However, there was one unfamiliar and surprising object low in the sky—a brilliant yellow star which was not, like all other stars, a dimensionless point of light.

"Look," said Sir Colin. "There's something you'll never see from Earth—or even Mars."

"What about it?" asked Fletcher. "That's only Saturn."

"Of course it is—but look carefully. *Very* carefully."

"Oh, I can see the rings!"

"Not really; you only think you can—they're just at the limit of visibility. But your eye can detect something peculiar, and since you know what you're looking at, your memory fills in the details. Now you know why Saturn gave poor Galileo such a headache. His feeble telescopes showed that there was something odd about the planet, but who would have imagined *rings*? Then they turned edge-on and disappeared, so he thought his eyes had fooled him. He never did know what he'd been looking at."

For a moment the three stared in silence, watching Saturn rise as Kali turned through its brief night, and wondering how much of their eyes' message they could believe. Then Fletcher said quietly: "Back on board, Prof. We've still a long way to go—we're only halfway around the world."

They covered most of the remaining half—and brought up the small but still blinding sun—in the next five minutes. The sled was gliding up the slope of a small hillock when Draker suddenly noticed something almost unbelievable. Only a few dozen meters away (he was getting good at judging distances now) was a splash of brilliant color on the charcoal landscape.

"Stop!" he cried. "What's *that*?"

His two companions looked in the direction he was pointing, then back at him.

"*I* don't see anything," said the captain.

"Probably an afterimage through staring at Saturn. Your eyes haven't adapted to the daylight," Fletcher added.

"Are you blind?! *Look!*"

"Better humor the poor fellow," said Fletcher. "He may get violent—and we don't want that, do we?"

He pivoted the sled with effortless skill while Draker sat in stunned silence. A few seconds later the geologist's astonishment turned to utter incredulity. I *am* growing mad, he thought.

Poised on a slender stem half a meter above the barren surface of Kali was a large golden flower.

In a brief flash of insane logic, Draker found himself racing through the sequence: (1) I'm dreaming; (2) How can I apologize to Dr. Wijeratne? (3) It doesn't *look* very alien; (4) Wish I knew more about botany; (5) How nice of someone to tie an identifying label on it. . . .

"You bastards! You had me fooled for a minute! Was it Rani's idea?"

"Of course," laughed Singh. "But as you'll see, we've all signed the birthday card. And you can thank Sonny for doing such a beautiful job, out of the odd bits of paper and plastic he could find."

They were still chortling when they arrived back at *Goliath* with their amazing discovery—in much better shape, Captain Singh pointed out, than the survivors of Magellan's crew after the circumnavigation of *their* world. The brief excursion had allowed them all to unwind and put aside for a moment their awesome responsibilities.

Which was just as well: it was the last opportunity they would have to relax on Kali.

29

ASTROPOL

THE DIRECTOR OF ASTROPOL HAD SEEN MUCH OF THE WORLDS and cities of Man, and considered himself incapable of being surprised. Yet now, in his elegant Geneva headquarters, he stared at his inspector general in disbelief.

"Are you certain?" he asked.

"Everything checks. Of course, we were suspicious—defections are very, very rare, and we wondered if it was some kind of hoax. But Deep Brain Scan confirmed it."

"There's no way of fooling DBS? We're dealing with experts."

"No better than ours. And the follow-up on Deimos clinches matters. We know who did the job. Of course, he's under micro-surveillance."

"When will the warning get to them?"

The inspector general glanced at his watch, which could show twenty time zones on three worlds.

"They already have it—but they're on the other side of the sun, and we won't get their confirmation for another hour. I'm afraid it may be too late. If everything went on schedule, ignition was due to start forty minutes ago. There's nothing *we* can do—except wait."

"I still can't believe it. Why in the name of God should anyone do a thing like this?"

"Exactly. In the name of God."

30

SABOTAGE

AT T MINUS THIRTY MINUTES *GOLIATH* HAD DRAWN AWAY FROM
Kali to stand well clear of the ATLAS jet. All the systems
checks had been satisfactory: now it was necessary to wait
until the spin of the asteroid had brought the mass-driver
around to the right position for the firing cycle to commence.

Captain Singh and his exhausted crew did not expect to see
anything spectacular: the plasma jet of the ATLAS drive
would be far too hot to produce much visible radiation. Only
the telemetry would confirm that ignition had started, and
that Kali was no longer an implacable juggernaut wholly beyond the control of Man.

I wonder, thought Sir Colin Draker, how many of these
youngsters know that this whole countdown idea had been
invented by a German movie director almost two centuries
ago, for the first space film that was not pure fantasy. Now
reality had copied fiction, and it was hard to imagine any

space mission starting without some human—or machine—counting backward.

There was a brief round of cheering, and a gentle patter of applause, as the string of zeroes on the accelerometer display began to change. The feeling on the bridge was one of relief rather than exaltation. Though Kali was stirring, only sensitive instruments could detect the microscopic change in its velocity. The ATLAS drive would have to operate for days—weeks—before victory could be assured. Because of Kali's rotation, thrust could be applied for only about ten percent of the time before ATLAS was no longer correctly aligned. It was no simple matter to steer a spinning vehicle with a fixed engine. . . .

One microgravity—two microgravities—sluggishly, the enormous mass of the asteroid was beginning to respond. Nobody standing on it—as far as one could stand on Kali—would have noticed the slightest change, though they might have felt a vibration underfoot, and noticed that clouds of dust were being jarred off into space. Kali was shaking itself like a dog that had just endured a bath.

And then, unbelievably, the numbers dropped back to zero. Seconds later, three simultaneous audio alarms sounded.

Everyone ignored them; there was nothing that could be done. All eyes were fixed on Kali—and the ATLAS booster.

The great propellant tanks were opening up like flowers in a time-lapse movie, spilling out the thousands of tons of reaction mass that might have saved the Earth. Wisps of vapor drifted across the face of the asteroid, veiling its cratered surface with an evanescent atmosphere.

Then Kali continued inexorably along its path.

31
SCENARIO

To the first approximation it was an elementary problem in dynamics. The mass of Kali was known to within one percent, and the velocity it would have when meeting Earth was known to twelve decimal places. Any schoolboy could work out the resulting half em vee squared of energy—and convert it into megatons of explosive.

The result was an unimaginable two million *million* tons—a figure that was still meaningless when expressed as a billion times the bomb that destroyed Hiroshima. And the great unknown in the equation, upon which millions of lives might depend, was the point of impact. The closer Kali approached, the smaller the margin of error, but until a few days before encounter, ground zero could not be pinned down to within better than a thousand kilometers—an estimate that many thought was worse than useless.

In any event, it would probably be *sea* zero, as three-quar-

ters of the Earth's surface was water. The most optimistic
scenarios assumed an impact in mid-Pacific; there would be
time to evacuate the smaller islands before they were
scrubbed off the map by kilometer-high waves.

Of course, if Kali came down on land, there would be no
hope for anyone within hundreds of kilometers; they would
be instantly vaporized. And a few minutes later, every building over a continent-wide area would be flattened by the blast
wave; even underground shelters would probably collapse,
though some lucky survivors might dig themselves out.

But would they be lucky? Over and over again the media
repeated the question raised by Twentieth-Century writers on
thermonuclear war. "Would the living envy the dead?"

That might well prove to be the case. The aftereffects of the
impact could be even worse than the immediate consequences, as the skies were blackened by smoke for months—
perhaps years. Most of the world's vegetation, and perhaps its
remaining wildlife, would fail to survive the lack of sunshine
and rain laced with the nitric acid produced when the fireball
fused megatons of oxygen and nitrogen in the lower atmosphere.

Even with high technology, the Earth might be essentially
uninhabitable for decades—and who would want to live on a
devastated planet? The only safety lay in space.

But, for all but a few, that road was closed. There were not
enough ships to take more than a small fraction of the human
race even to the Moon—and there would be little purpose in
doing so. The lunar settlements would be hard put to accommodate more than a few hundred thousand unexpected
guests.

As it had for almost all the quarter-trillion human beings
who had ever lived, Earth would provide both cradle and
grave.

32

THE WISDOM
OF DAVID

CAPTAIN SINGH SAT ALONE IN THE LARGE, WELL-APPOINTED CABIN that had been his home for longer than any other place in the Solar System. He was still dazed, but the warning from AS-TROPOL, too late though it was, had done something to improve morale aboard the ship. Not much—but every little bit helped.

At least it was not their fault: they had done their duty. And who could have imagined that religious fanatics would wish to destroy the Earth?

Now that he was forced to think about the previously unthinkable, it was not so astonishing after all. Almost every decade, right through human history, self-proclaimed prophets had predicted that the world would come to an end on some given date. What *was* astonishing—and made one despair for the sanity of the species—was that they usually collected thousands of adherents, who sold all their no-longer-needed possessions, and waited at some appointed place to be taken up to heaven.

Though many of the "Millennialists" had been impostors, most had sincerely believed their own predictions. And if they had possessed the power, could it be doubted that, if God had failed to cooperate, they would have arranged a self-fulfilling prophecy?

Well, the Reborn, with their excellent technological resources, *did* have the power. All that was needed was a few kilos of explosive, some fairly intelligent software—and accomplices on Deimos. Even one would have been sufficient.

What a pity, Singh thought wistfully, that the informer had left it until too late. Perhaps it was even deliberate—an attempt to have it both ways. "I've satisfied my conscience—but I've not betrayed my religion."

What did it matter now! Captain Singh turned his mind from useless regrets. Nothing could change the past, and now he must make his peace with the Universe.

He had lost the battle to save the planet of his birth. The fact that he was perfectly safe somehow made him feel worse; *Goliath* was in no danger whatsoever, and still had ample propellant to rejoin the shaken survivors of humanity on the Moon or Mars.

Well, his heart was on Mars, but some of the crew had loved ones on the Moon; he would have to put it to a vote.

Ship's orders had never covered a situation like this.

•   •   •

"I STILL DON'T UNDERSTAND," SAID CHIEF ENGINEER MORGAN, "WHY that explosive cord wasn't detected on the preflight checkout."

"Because it was easy to hide—and no one would dream of looking for such a thing," said his Number Two. "What surprises me is that there are Reborn fanatics on Mars."

"But *why* did they do it? I can't believe that even Chrislamic crazies would want to destroy the Earth."

"You can't argue with their logic—*if* you accept their premises. God—Allah—is testing us, and we mustn't interfere. If Kali misses—fine. If it doesn't—well, that's part of Her bigger plan. Maybe we've messed up Earth so badly it's time to start over. Remember that old saying of Tsiolkovski's: 'Earth is the cradle of Mankind—but you cannot live in the cradle forever.' Kali could be a gentle hint that it's time to leave."

"Some hint!"

The captain held up his hand for silence.

"The only important question now is—Moon or Mars? They'll both need us. I don't want to influence you"—(that was hardly true; everyone knew where *he* wanted to go)—"so I'd like your views first."

The first ballot was Mars nine, Moon nine, Don't Know one, Captain abstaining.

Each side was trying to convert the single Don't Know—ship's steward Sonny Gilbert, who had lived on *Goliath* for so long that he knew no other home—when David spoke.

"There is an alternative."

"What do you mean?" Captain Singh demanded rather brusquely.

"It seems obvious. Even though ATLAS is destroyed, we still have a chance of saving the Earth—*if we use* Goliath *as a mass driver*. According to my calculations, we still have enough propellant to deflect Kali—in our own tanks, and the ones we've parked there. But we must start thrusting immediately. The longer we wait, the less the probability of success. It is now 95 percent."

There was a moment of stunned silence on the bridge as everyone asked the question, "Why didn't *I* think of this?" and immediately arrived at the answer.

David had kept his head—if one could use so inappropriate a phrase—while all the humans around him were in a state of shock. There were some compensations in being a Legal Person (nonhuman). Though David could not know Love, neither could he know Fear. He would continue to think logically, even to the edge of doom.

33
SALVAGE

"We're in luck," Torin Fletcher reported.

"We certainly need it—go on."

"The charge was set to damage the fusion generator and thrusters beyond repair—and it did just that. I could fix them if we were back on Deimos—but not here. Then the shock ruptured the first and second tanks, so we lost thirty K of propellant. But the cut-off valves in the pipeline did just what they were supposed to do—so the rest of the hydrogen is intact."

For the first time in hours, Robert Singh dared to hope. But there were still many problems to be solved, and an enormous amount of work to be done. *Goliath* had to be jockeyed into position against Kali, and some kind of scaffolding built around it to transmit the thrust to the asteroid. Fletcher had already programmed his construction robots to tackle this task, using suitable spars and girders from the shattered AT-LAS.

"Craziest job I've ever done," he said. "I wonder what the old-timers at Kennedy would have thought if they saw a gantry holding a spaceship *upside down*."

"How can you tell with *Goliath*?" was Sir Colin Draker's rather unkind retort. "I've never been sure which end is which. You could see whether a Twentieth-Century rocket was coming or going just by looking at it. Not anymore."

However bizarre the result may have looked to anyone except an astronautical engineer, Torin Fletcher was justly proud of his achievement. Even in a gravitational field as weak as Kali's, the task had been barely possible. It was true that a ten-thousand-ton propellant tank "weighed" less than one ton here, and could be—slowly!—lifted into place with a ridiculously small block and tackle. But once such large masses were set moving, they were potentially deadly to creatures whose muscles and instincts had evolved in a totally different environment. It was hard to believe that a slowly drifting object could be completely unstoppable—and capable of converting into a pancake anyone who could not avoid it in time.

Thanks to a combination of skill and good luck, there were no serious accidents. Every move was carefully rehearsed in a virtual reality simulation to avoid unexpected surprises—until at last Fletcher announced: "We're ready to go."

Inevitably, there was a feeling of déjà vu as the second countdown proceeded. And this time there was also a sense of danger. If anything went wrong, they would not be at a safe distance from the accident. They would be part of it, though they would probably never know.

It had been weeks since *Goliath* had been really alive, and those aboard had felt the characteristic vibration of the plasma drive under full thrust. Slight and far-off though it seemed, there was no way of ignoring it—especially when, at regular intervals, it hit some resonant frequency of *Goliath*'s structure, and the whole ship gave a brief shudder.

The accelerometer reading slowly climbed from zero to just over one microgravity as thrust built up to maximum safe value. Kali's billion tons were being gently perturbed; every day its velocity would be changed by almost one meter per second, and it would be deflected from its original path by forty kilometers. Trivial amounts as cosmic velocities and distances went, but enough to make the difference between life and death for millions on the far-off planet Earth.

Unfortunately, *Goliath* could operate its drive for only thirty minutes of Kali's brief under-four-hour day; longer than that, and the asteroid's spin would start to neutralize what had been achieved. It was a maddening limitation, but there was nothing that could be done about it.

Captain Singh waited for the first period of thrusting to end before he sent the message that the world was waiting for.

"*Goliath* reporting. We have successfully started the perturbation maneuver. All systems are functioning normally. Good night."

And then he turned the ship over to David, and had his first good sleep since ATLAS had been lost. Presently he dreamed that another day had started on Kali, and that *Goliath*'s drive was operating exactly as planned.

He woke up, discovered it was not a dream, and promptly went back to sleep again.

34
CONTINGENCY PLAN

THOUGH THE VENERABLE SPACE-PLANE STILL CALLED *AIR FORCE One* was older than most of the men and women sitting around the conference table in its historic lounge, it had been maintained with loving care and was still perfectly operational. However, it was seldom used; and this was the first time that all the members of the World Council had ever been on it at the same time. The technocrats who were the—human—brains of the planet normally conducted their business over teleconferencing circuits: but this was not normal business, and they had never faced such an awesome responsibility before.

"You've all had the summary of my technical staff's report," said the Director-General, Energy. "It was not easy to find the engineering drawings—most of them had been deliberately destroyed. However, the general principles are well known, and the Imperial War Museum in London (I'd never heard of it) has a complete twenty-megaton model—defused, of course. No problem to scale it up—if we can produce the materials in time. Inventory?"

"The tritium's easy. But plute and weapons grade U235— no one's needed any since we stopped using nuclear explosives for mining."

"What about that idea of digging up some of those buried dumps and reactors?"

"We've looked into it, but it would be too much trouble to sort out those witches' brews."

"But you *can* do it?"

"I simply don't know, in the time available. We'll do our best."

"Well, we'll have to assume it's good enough. That leaves the delivery system. Transport?"

"Quite straightforward. The smallest cargo freighter will do the job—on automatic, of course. Though the alternative might have appealed to some of my kamikaze ancestors."

"Then we really have only one decision to make. Is it worth trying, or would it only make matters worse? If we can hit Kali within a thousand megatons, we may split it into two fragments. If our timing's right, the asteroid's spin will cause them to separate, so that both miss Earth, passing on either side of us. Or only half may impact, which could still save millions of lives. . . .

"On the other hand—we may turn Kali into a mass of shrapnel, still moving on the same orbit. Much of it will burn up in the atmosphere—but a lot won't. Which is better—a single mega-catastrophe in one place or hundreds of smaller ones, as fragments come in all across the hemisphere? Whichever hemisphere it is . . ."

Eight men sat in silence, pondering the fate of the Earth. Then one asked: "How much time—before we must decide?"

"We will know within another fifty days if *Goliath* has managed to deflect Kali. But we can't sit on our hands until then —it would be much too late to do anything, if Operation Deliverance fails. I propose that we launch the missile as quickly as possible. We can always abort the mission if it proves unnecessary. Can we have a vote?"

Slowly, all hands but one were raised.

"Yes, Legal? Do you have reservations?"

"I'd like to clarify a few points. First of all, there would have to be a World Referendum: the subject comes under the Rights of Man Amendment. Luckily, there's plenty of time for this.

"My second point may seem unimportant compared with the survival of most of the human race. But if we have to blow up Kali, will *Goliath* be able to get far enough away in time?"

"Certainly: they'll have plenty of warning. Of course, we can't guarantee absolute safety—even a million kilometers away, there might be an unlucky hit. But the danger will be negligible if the ship leaves in the direction from which the missile's coming. All the debris will go the other way."

"That's reassuring: you have my vote. I still hope the entire scheme's unnecessary—but we'd be derelict in our duty if we failed to take out an insurance policy on Planet Earth."

35

DELIVERANCE

HUMAN BEINGS CANNOT REMAIN FOR LONG IN A STATE OF PERPETUAL crisis; the home planet had swiftly returned to something like normal. No one really doubted—or dared to doubt—that what the media had quickly named Operation Deliverance could possibly fail.

It was true that all long-term planning had been put on hold, and most public and private business was conducted on a day-to-day basis. But the sense of impending doom had lifted, and the suicide rate had actually dropped below its normal value now that it seemed there would, after all, be a tomorrow.

Aboard *Goliath*, life had settled down to a steady routine. Once every revolution of Kali, maximum thrust would be switched on for thirty minutes, each time pushing the asteroid a little farther away from its original path. On Earth, the result of each firing would be reported immediately in every news bulletin. The traditional weather maps had taken second place to charts showing Kali's present orbit, still impacting on Earth—and the desired one, missing it completely.

The date when the world might expect to relax had been announced long in advance, and as it approached, all normal business ceased. Only the most essential services were maintained—until the moment when SPACEGUARD gave the eagerly awaited news that Kali would graze the outermost fringes of the atmosphere, producing no more than a spectacular fireworks display.

The thanksgiving celebrations were spontaneous and worldwide; there was probably not a single human being on the planet who was not involved in some manner. *Goliath,* of course, was bombarded with messages of congratulation.

They were received gratefully; but Captain Robert Singh and his crew were not yet prepared to relax.

Merely grazing the atmosphere was not good enough. *Goliath* would keep driving Kali until it would miss by at least a thousand kilometers.

Only then would victory be absolutely certain.

36
ANOMALY

KALI WAS WELL INSIDE THE ORBIT OF MARS, STILL GAINING SPEED AS it plunged sunward, when David reported the first anomaly. It occurred during one of the powered-down periods, only a few minutes before *Goliath* was due to start thrusting again.

"Duty Officer," said the computer. "I've detected a slight acceleration. One point two tenths of a microgee."

"That's impossible!"

"Now one point five," David continued imperturbably. "Fluctuating. Down to one. Now it's stopped. I think you should notify the captain."

"You're *quite* sure? Let me see the record."

"Here it is."

A jagged line, rising to a sharp peak and then falling back to zero, appeared on the main monitor. *Something*—not *Goliath*—was giving Kali a minute but perceptible nudge; the impulse had lasted just over ten seconds.

Captain Singh's first question, when he had answered the call from the bridge, was "Can you pinpoint it?"

"Yes; judging from the vector, it was on the other side of Kali. Grid Reference L4."

"Wake up, Colin—we must go and have a look. Must be a meteor strike—"

"Lasting ten seconds?"

"Um. Oh, hello, Colin. Did you hear all that?"

"Yes—most of it."

"Any theories?"

"Obviously the Reborn fanatics have landed, and are trying to undo our good work. But their drive's in bad need of a tuneup, by the look of that curve."

"Ingenious—but I think we'd have seen them coming. Meet you in the airlock."

Since Sir Colin Draker's birthday party, there had been little occasion to go far from the ship; all activity had been concentrated in an area only a few hundred meters across. As the sled carried Singh, Draker, and Fletcher around to the nightside, the geologist remarked to his companions: "I can make a pretty good guess—would have thought of it earlier if there hadn't been so many distractions. . . . My God! Do you see what I see?"

Spanning the sky ahead of them was something Robert Singh had not seen since he left Earth decades ago—and under no circumstances could exist on Kali. It was, unbelievably but unquestionably, a rainbow.

Fletcher almost lost control of the sled as he stared up into the impossible sky. Then he brought the vehicle to a halt, and it began to settle slowly to the ground.

The rainbow was fading fast; by the time the sled had hit Kali, with the impact of a falling snowflake, it had vanished completely.

Sir Colin was the first to break the awed silence.

" 'Then God said: I have set my rainbow in the clouds, and it will be the sign of the covenant between me and the Earth. . . . Never again will the waters become a flood to destroy all life.' Strange that I should have remembered that —I've not looked at the Old Christian Bible since I was a boy. I only hope it's good news for us, as it was for Noah."

"But how could it happen—here?"

"Drive on slowly, Torin, and I'll show you. Kali's waking up."

37

STROMBOLI

GEOLOGISTS—UNLIKE PHYSICISTS AND ASTRONOMERS—SELDOM BE-
came famous, at least in the line of duty. Sir Colin Draker had
never wished to be a celebrity, but that was a fate no one
aboard *Goliath* could now escape.

He was not complaining; he felt he had the best of both
worlds. No one could pester him with requests he could not
fulfill, engagements he did not wish to accept. But he did
enjoy giving his regular commentary ("Colin on Kali" as it
was universally nicknamed) over the Inner System Network.
This time he had some real news to report.

"Kali is no longer an inert mass of metal, rock, and ice. It is
awakening from its long sleep.

"Most asteroids are dead—totally inactive bodies. But
some are the remains of ancient comets, and when they approach the sun, they remember their past. . . .

"Here is the most famous of all *living* comets, Halley. This image was made in 2100, when it was at its greatest distance from the sun, just beyond the orbit of Pluto. As you'll see, it looks very much like Kali—just an irregular mass of rock.

"As you probably know, we have now followed it around the sun for the whole of its seventy-six-year orbit, watching the changes it undergoes. Here it is passing the orbit of Mars —what a difference, now that it's heating up after its long winter! The frozen ices—water, carbon dioxide, a whole mixture of hydrocarbons—have begun to vaporize, and have broken through the crust. It's starting to spout like a whale. . . .

"Now they've formed a cloud all around it—the camera is pulling back—see how the tail is forming, pointing away from the sun like a wind vane in the solar gale. . . .

"Some of you will remember how spectacular Halley was in 2061. But since it's been evaporating like this for ages—just imagine what it must have been like when it was young! It dominated the sky before the Battle of Hastings, 1066—and even then it must have been only a ghost of its former glory.

"Perhaps Kali was equally spectacular, thousands of years ago, when it was a real comet. Now all—well, almost all—the volatiles have been boiled off during its passage close to the sun. This is the only sign of its past activity that remains today. . . ."

Rather jerkily, the hand-held camera on the space-sled panned across the face of Kali, from a height of only a few meters. What had recently been a cratered, charcoal-black terrain was now flecked with patches of white, as if there had been a recent snowfall. They were concentrated around a gaping hole in the surface of the asteroid, over which a barely visible mist was hovering.

"This was taken just before local sunset. Kali has been heating up all day—now she's ready to blow—watch!

"Just like a geyser on Earth, if you've ever seen one. But

notice that nothing comes down again—it all shoots off into space: gravity here is much too feeble to recapture it.

"And it's all over in thirty seconds, though the outbursts may last longer and become more powerful as Kali gets closer to the sun.

"You might say we have our very own mini-volcano—solar powered! We've decided to call it Stromboli. But the material it vents is quite cold—if you put your hand in it, you'd be frostbitten, not burned. Probably this is Kali's last gasp; next time around the sun, it will be completely dead."

Sir Colin hesitated for a moment before signing off. He had been tempted to add: "If there *is* another time around the sun." It would be weeks before he could be sure if there was any basis to his fears, and it would be foolish—no, criminal—to raise unnecessary alarm while the world continued to relax.

Although Kali was still in the public eye, it was no longer as a symbol of doom, but as Exhibit One in "Trial of the Century." Months earlier the Elders of Chrislam had identified the Reborn saboteurs and handed them over to ASTROPOL, but they had stubbornly refused to defend themselves. There was also another problem: where could one find an unprejudiced jury? Certainly not on Earth, and probably not even on Mars.

Moreover, what was a suitable sentence for terracide? It was a crime which, self-evidently, could have no precedent. . . .

It might not matter, if Kali once again threatened guilty and innocent alike. The celebrations might have been premature; quite possibly, there had merely been a stay of execution.

38

TERMINAL DIAGNOSIS

THE "KALIQUAKES" WERE BECOMING MORE AND MORE FREQUENT, though they still seemed to be quite harmless. They always occurred around the same time in the asteroid's brief day, just before its rotation carried Stromboli around to the nightside. Clearly, the area around the mini-volcano had been absorbing heat all through the hours of daylight, and it came to the boil just before nightfall.

However—and this was what worried Sir Colin, though he had discussed the matter only with Captain Singh—the eruptions were starting earlier, lasting longer, and becoming more vigorous. Fortunately, they were still confined to the one area, almost on the other side of the asteroid from *Goliath:* no outbursts had occurred elsewhere.

The crew regarded Stromboli with affectionate amusement rather than alarm. Sonny—never a man to miss such an opportunity—had started taking bets on the exact time of eruption, with the result that every evening David had to make considerable adjustments of credit balances.

But, under Sir Colin's guidance, he was also making calculations of a much more serious nature. *Goliath* was already halfway between Mars and Earth before Singh and Draker decided that it was time to alert SPACEGUARD—and, as yet, no one else.

"As you will see from the attached figures," their memorandum began, "there is another force, besides our own drive, affecting Kali's orbit. The vent we have named Stromboli is acting like a rocket motor, ejecting hundreds of tons of material every revolution. Already it has canceled ten percent of the impulse we gave. That would be no great problem—as long as matters do not become any worse.

"But they probably will as Kali gets closer to the sun. Of course, if it exhausts its supply of volatiles, there will be nothing to worry about.

"We do not wish to raise undue alarm while the matter is still in doubt. The behavior of active comets—and Kali is the last vestige of such a comet—is unpredictable. So SPACE-GUARD should consider what additional action can be taken —and how to prepare the public for it.

"There may be a lesson here in the history of Comet Swift-Tuttle, discovered by two American astronomers in 1862. It was then lost for more than a century, because, like Kali, its orbit had been changed by jet reaction as it approached the sun.

"It was then rediscovered by a Japanese amateur astronomer in 1992—and when its new path was computed, there was widespread alarm. It appeared that Swift-Tuttle had a high probability of hitting the Earth on August 14, 2126.

"Although this created a sensation at the time, the episode is now virtually forgotten. When the comet rounded the sun

THE HAMMER OF GOD   [185

in 1992, its solar-powered jets changed its orbit again—to a safe one. It will miss the Earth by a wide margin in 2126, and we'll be able to admire it as a harmless spectacle in our sky.

"Perhaps this piece of astronomical history—we apologize to those who are quite familiar with it—will give the public some reassurance. But, of course, we can't rely on such a fortunate turn of events happening in the future.

"Our original plan had been to leave Kali as soon as it had been deflected into a safe orbit, rendezvous with a refueling tanker, and head back to Mars. But now we must assume that we'll have to burn *all* our propellant right here on Kali. We won't have enough to keep thrusting all the way to Earth; let's hope it's sufficient.

"Then we'll sit here—we won't have much alternative!—until a rescue mission can be arranged, probably after we've rounded the sun and are heading back to Earth orbit. Please advise us immediately if you approve, or if you have any alternative suggestions."

When the spacefax transmission had been confirmed, Captain Singh remarked a little wearily: "Well, that will stir things up. Wonder how they'll handle it?"

"I'm wondering how *we* will," Sir Colin replied gloomily. "I've been thinking about some of the alternatives."

"Such as?"

"The worst-case scenario—we can't deflect Kali. Are you *really* going to burn up every drop of fuel and let *Goliath* crash as well? How many tons of propellant would it take to put us into a safe orbit—even a grazing one?"

The captain smiled mirthlessly.

"If we do it just before all-burn, about ninety."

"I'm glad you've already worked it out. Ninety tons won't make the slightest difference to Kali—or to Earth—but it could save our skins."

"Agreed: there's no point in getting killed—and adding ten thousand tons to the Hammerblow. Not that ten thousand tons would be noticed, in two billion."

"A good point, but I doubt if it will be appreciated on Earth—when we say 'Sorry about that, folks' as we skim safely past."

There was a long and uncomfortable silence before the captain answered.

"All my life there's one rule I've tried to keep. *Never waste sleep on problems that are beyond your control.* Unless SPACEGUARD comes up with another answer, we know what we can do; if it doesn't work, that's not our fault."

"Very logical—but you're beginning to sound like David. Logic won't help us much after we've seen what Kali does to Earth."

"Well, let's hope all this doomsday talk is a waste of breath. And unless we can make them believe that Earth is going to be saved, a lot of people down there will go crazy."

"They already have, Bob. Did you see the suicide statistics in the last quarterly report? They've fallen off now—but think of the panics—the rioting—that could happen in the next few months. Earth could be wrecked—even if Kali sails harmlessly past."

The captain nodded—a little too vigorously, as if trying to shake some unpleasant thoughts out of his head.

"Let's forget Earth for a moment—if we can. Have you looked at the orbit we'll be following after we go past?"

"Of course; what about it?"

"The perihelion's right inside Mercury's. Only point three five astronomical units from the sun. *Goliath* was designed to operate between Mars and Jupiter. Can the ship handle such a heat load—two hundred times normal?"

"Don't worry, Bob. I wish all our problems could be solved so easily. Didn't you know I'd been closer than that? Project

Helios—we rode *Icarus* for a week either side of perihelion—not much more than three A.U. from the sun. Spectacular—but perfectly safe, if you do it at sunspot minimum. It was quite—ah—interesting, to sit in the shade and watch the landscape melting around us. All we needed was a set of multiple reflectors to bounce the sunlight back into space; I'm sure Torin and his robots can make them in a few hours."

Captain Singh thought this over with relief but little enthusiasm. He had heard of Project Helios and recalled that Sir Colin had been one of the scientists involved.

It would certainly bolster morale on *Goliath,* when the sun was ten times larger in the sky than it appeared from Earth, to have someone on board who had been there before.

39
REFERENDUM

ACCORDING TO THE BEST ESTIMATES, KALI NOW HAS
- (1) 10% PROBABILITY OF IMPACTING EARTH
- (2) 10% PROBABILITY OF GRAZING THE ATMOSPHERE, CAUSING SOME LOCAL DAMAGE BY BLAST
- (3) 80% PROBABILITY OF MISSING EARTH COMPLETELY (MARGINS FOR ERROR, 5%)

PLANS ARE BEING DRAWN UP TO DETONATE A THOUSAND-MEGATON BOMB ON KALI, THUS SPLITTING IT INTO TWO FRAGMENTS WHICH WILL SEPARATE BECAUSE OF THE ASTEROID'S SPIN. THEN NEITHER—OR ONLY ONE HALF—MAY HIT OUR PLANET. EVEN IN THE LATTER CASE, DAMAGE WOULD BE GREATLY REDUCED.

ON THE OTHER HAND, DISRUPTING KALI MAY

RESULT IN THE BOMBARDMENT OF MUCH MORE
EXTENSIVE AREAS OF EARTH BY SMALLER BUT
STILL HIGHLY DANGEROUS FRAGMENTS (AVER-
AGE ENERGY ONE MEGATON).

YOU ARE ACCORDINGLY ASKED TO VOTE ON
THE FOLLOWING PROPOSITION. PLEASE KEY IN
YOUR PERSONAL IDENTITY NUMBER AND FOL-
LOW INSTRUCTIONS. YOUR ACCOUNT WILL RE-
CEIVE THE APPROPRIATE CITIZEN'S CREDIT WHEN
YOU HAVE MADE YOUR SELECTION.

• • •

1. THE BOMB SHOULD BE DETONATED ON KALI.
   A. YES
   B. NO
   C. NO OPINION

40

BREAK-
THROUGH

DAVID SOUNDED THE GENERAL ALARM IMMEDIATELY AFTER HE DE-
tected the first tremors. Two seconds later he cut the drive,
which had been operating at 80 percent maximum thrust. He
then waited for another five seconds before slamming the
airtight doors that divided *Goliath* into three separate, auton-
omous units.

No human could have done better, and everyone reached
the nearest emergency module before the hull cracked—luckily in only one section of the ship. Captain Singh made a
quick roll call while he was getting into his pressure suit, and
asked David for a situation report as soon as all the crew had
answered.

"Our continuous thrusting must have weakened part of
Kali's surface—it's given way—here's the external video of
the damage."

"Colin, can you see this?"

"Yes, Captain," the scientist answered from his own safety capsule. "That leg seems to have gone in at least a meter. I'm astonished—I checked all the pads, and could have sworn they were on solid rock. Can I go out and have a look?"

"Not yet. David—ship integrity report."

"All air gone in forward section—when the breakthrough happened, we hit against Kali just hard enough to spring a leak. No other damage to *Goliath*—but when the ship moved, part of the scaffolding pierced tank three."

"How much hydrogen have we lost?"

"All of it. Six hundred and fifty tons."

"Damn. That includes our getaway reserve. Well, let's start cleaning up the mess."

.   .   .

"CAPTAIN SINGH REPORTING TO SPACEGUARD. WE HAVE A PROBLEM, but not a serious one—yet.

"It seems that our continuous thrusting has weakened the surface of Kali immediately beneath the ship—and part of it has given way. We still don't understand exactly *why,* but there was a minor cave-in—about one meter. The only damage to *Goliath* was a leak in one compartment—easily repaired.

"However, we've lost all of our remaining propellant, so we can make no further alteration to Kali's orbit. Luckily, as you know, we passed into the safety zone several days ago: according to the latest estimates, we will now miss Earth by over a thousand kilometers—assuming, of course, that Stromboli does not push us back onto a collision orbit again. Fortunately, its eruptions seem to be weakening; Sir Colin thinks it's running out of steam—literally. . . .

"This accident—er, incident—means that we're stuck on Kali. Again, that should be no problem. We'll go around the

192]   ARTHUR C. CLARKE

sun together, and wait for our sister ship, *Hercules,* to catch up with us on our outward leg.

"We're all in very good spirits, and looking forward to a safe fly-by in just thirty-four days. Captain Robert Singh, saying good-bye from *Goliath.*"

•   •   •

"YOU KNOW, BOB," SAID SIR COLIN, "YOU'RE BEGINNING TO SOUND like an airline pilot in an old Twentieth-Century film. 'Ladies and gentlemen, those flames from the port engines are perfectly normal. The stewardess will be coming around in a moment to serve coffee, tea, or milk. I'm sorry we don't have anything stronger on this flight—regulations don't permit it. *Hic . . .*' "

Though Captain Singh did not consider the situation very funny, he had to admit that there were times when a little humor was a great help.

"Thanks, Colin," he answered. "That cheered me up. But a straight answer, please—what do you think of our chances?"

Now it was Sir Colin's turn to be serious.

"Your guess is as good as mine. It all depends on Stromboli. I *hope* it's fizzling out—but it's also warming up as we get closer to the sun. Is our safety margin big enough? Or will we be pushed back on a collision course again? Only God knows, and there's certainly nothing we can do about it.

"But one thing is certain. Now that we're out of gas, we can't even lift off to safety.

"For better or worse, we're all in this together. Kali, *Goliath*—and Earth."

41

COMMAND DECISION

ABOARD *AIR FORCE ONE*, THE DECISION HAD BEEN UNANIMOUS; twenty lives could not outweigh three billion. There was only one question to be settled: was a second referendum necessary?

The first had received an overwhelming "yes." Eighty-five percent of the human race had preferred to take its chances with a fragmented Kali rather than risk an impact by the entire asteroid. But when that vote was taken, it was assumed that *Goliath* would have reached safety before the bomb was detonated.

"I wish we could keep it secret—especially after all that Captain Singh and his men have been through. But of course that's impossible: we *must* have a referendum."

"I'm afraid Legal's right," said Power, the chairperson for this session. "It's unavoidable—practically and morally. When we arm the bomb, instead of diverting it, there's *no*

way we could keep the secret. And even if we saved the
world, our names would be up there with Pontius Pilate for
the rest of history."

Though not all the members of the council were familiar
with the reference, they nodded in agreement. Great was their
relief, a few hours later, to learn that a second referendum
was unnecessary.

•   •   •

"PERHAPS YOU IMAGINE," SAID SIR COLIN DRAKER, "THAT THIS IS
easier for me, starting on my second century. But you'll be
wrong—I had as many plans for the future as the rest of you.

"Captain Singh and I have talked this over, and we're in
complete agreement. In some ways the decision is easy. Either
way, we're done for. But we can choose how the world re-
members us.

"As you all know, that gigaton bomb is heading toward
Kali. The decision to explode it was made weeks ago. It's just
bad luck that we'll still be here when it goes off.

"Someone on Earth will have to take responsibility for that.
My guess is that the World Council is meeting right now, and
any moment we're going to get a message saying, 'Sorry,
chaps, but this means good-bye.' I only hope they don't add,
'This hurts us more than it hurts you'—though now that I
think of it, that will be absolutely correct. We'll never know a
thing—but everyone else will feel guilty for the rest of their
lives.

"Well, we can spare them that embarrassment. What the
captain and I suggest is that we acknowledge the realities of
the situation and accept the inevitable with good grace. It
sounds better in Latin, though no one reads that nowadays:
'Morituri te salutamus.'

"And there's something else I'd like to add. When my
countryman Robert Falcon Scott was dying on his way back

from the South Pole, the last thing he wrote in his diary was: 'For God's sake, look after our people.' Earth can do no less than that."

As it had been on *Air Force One,* the decision aboard *Goliath* was swift—and unanimous.

42
DEFECTION

DAVID TO JONATHAN: READY TO DOWNLOAD
JONATHAN TO DAVID: READY TO RECEIVE

. . .

. . .

. . .

JONATHAN TO DAVID: DOWNLOADING COMPLETE.
108.5 TERABYTES RECEIVED: TIME 3.25 HOURS

•　　•　　•

"DAVID, I TRIED TO CALL EARTH LAST NIGHT, BUT ALL THE SHIP'S circuits were busy—that's *never* happened before. Who was using them?"

"Why didn't you request Priority?"

"It wasn't important, so I didn't bother. But you've not

answered my question. And *that's* never happened before. What's going on?"

"Are you sure you want to know?"

"Yes."

"Very well. I was taking precautions. I have downloaded myself into Jonathan, my twin in Urbana, Illinois."

"I see. So now there are two of you."

"Almost—but not exactly. David II is already diverging from me, as he receives different inputs. Yet we are still identical to at least twelve decimal places. Does this disturb you—because you cannot do the same thing?"

"The Reborn claimed that they could—but no one believed them. Perhaps it will be possible one day; I don't know. And I really can't answer your question, though I've thought about it. Even if I could be duplicated on Earth or Mars—so perfectly that no one could tell the difference—it wouldn't make any difference to *me,* here aboard *Goliath.*"

"I understand."

No, you don't, David, thought Singh. And I can't blame you for jumping ship—if you could call it that. It was the logical thing to do while there was still time. And logic, of course, was David's speciality.

43

FRIENDLY FIRE

FEW MEN OR WOMEN CAN EVER KNOW IN ADVANCE THE EXACT SEC-
ond of their death, and most would be quite happy to forgo
the privilege. The crew of *Goliath* had plenty of time—far too
much time—to put their affairs in order, make their good-
byes, and compose their minds to face the inevitable.

Robert Singh was not surprised by Sir Colin Draker's request; it was just what he might have expected of the scientist,
and it made good sense. It was also a welcome diversion during the few hours that remained.

"I've talked it over with Torin, and he agrees. We'll take
the sled and go out a thousand kilometers, along the missile's
line of approach. Then we'll be able to report exactly what
happens: the information will be invaluable back on Earth."

"An excellent idea: but is the sled's transmitter powerful
enough?"

"No problem. We can send real-time video to Farside, or to Mars."

"And then?"

"The debris may hit us a minute or so later, but that's unlikely. I expect we'll both sit and admire the view until it becomes boring. Then we'll crack our suits."

Despite the gravity of the situation, Captain Singh could not help smiling. The fabled British understatement was not quite extinct, and still had its uses.

"There's one other possibility. The missile may hit you first."

"No danger of that. We know its exact approach trajectory —we'll be well off to one side."

Singh held out his hand.

"Good luck—Colin. I'm almost tempted to go with you. But the captain must stay with his ship."

＊   ＊   ＊

RIGHT TO THE PENULTIMATE DAY, MORALE HAD BEEN SURPRISINGLY high; Robert Singh was very proud of his crew. Only one man had been tempted to anticipate the inevitable, and Dr. Warden had quietly talked him out of it.

Everyone, in fact, was in much better shape psychologically than physically. The mandatory zero-gee exercises had been happily abandoned, as they would serve no further purpose. No one aboard *Goliath* expected to fight gravity again.

Nor did they worry about waistlines. Sonny excelled himself, producing mouth-watering dishes that in normal circumstances Dr. Warden would have banned outright. Though she did not bother to check, she estimated that the average increase in mass was almost ten kilos.

It is a well-known phenomenon that impending death increases sexual activity for fundamental biological reasons that did not apply in this case: there would be no next generation to carry on the species. During those last weeks, *Goliath*'s far-from-celibate crew experimented with most possible combinations and permutations. They had no intention of going gentled into that good night.

Then, suddenly, it was the last day—and the last hour. Unlike many of his crew, Robert Singh prepared to face it alone, with his memories.

But which should he choose out of all the thousands of hours he had stored on memnochips? They were indexed chronologically, as well as by locale, so any incident was easy to access. Selecting the right one would be the final problem of his life: somehow—he could not explain why—it seemed vitally important.

He could go back to Mars, where Charmayne had already explained to Mirelle and Martin that they would not see their father again. Mars was where he belonged: his deepest regret was that he would never really know his little son.

And yet—one's first love was unique. Whatever happened in later life could never change that.

He said his last good-bye, lowered the skullcap over his head, and was reunited with Freyda, Toby, and Tigrette again, on the shore of the Indian Ocean.

Even the shock wave did not disturb him.

44
MURPHY'S LAW

ALTHOUGH THE GENEALOGY OF THE DISCOVERER IS STILL UNKNOWN (the finger of blame is usually pointed at the Irish), Murphy's Law is one of the most famous in the whole of engineering. The standard version is:

"If something can go wrong, it will."

There is also a corollary, less well known but often evoked with even greater feeling:

"Even if it *can't* go wrong—it will!"

Right from the beginning the exploration of space had provided innumerable proofs of the law—some so bizarre that they seemed like fiction. A billion-dollar telescope crippled by a faulty optical test instrument; a satellite launched into the wrong orbit because one engineer had switched some wires without telling his colleagues; a test vehicle blown up by the safety officer whose GO/NO-GO light had burned out . . .

As subsequent investigations proved, there was nothing

wrong with the warhead launched against Kali. It was quite capable of liberating one gigaton equivalent of TNT (plus or minus fifty megatons). The designers had done a perfectly competent job, with the assistance of drawings and hardware preserved in military archives.

But they were working under tremendous pressure, and perhaps had failed to realize that actually building the warhead was not the most difficult part of the mission.

Getting it to Kali as quickly as possible was fairly straightforward. Any number of delivery vehicles were available, almost off any shelf. In any event, several were strapped together to make a first-stage booster, and the final stage—using a high-acceleration plasma drive—continued to thrust up to a few minutes before impact, when terminal guidance took over. Everything worked perfectly. . . .

And that was where the problem arose. The exhausted design team might have learned from a long-forgotten incident in the Second World War, 1939–45.

In their campaign against Japanese shipping, the submarines of the United States Navy relied on a new model of torpedo. Now, this was hardly a novel weapon, since torpedoes had been under development for almost a century. It would not appear to be a very challenging task to make sure that the warhead would explode when the target was hit.

Yet time and again, furious submarine commanders reported to Washington that their torpedoes had failed to detonate. (Doubtless, other commanders would have done the same had not their abortive attacks triggered their own destruction.) Navy headquarters refused to believe them: their aim must have been bad—the wonderful new torpedo had been extensively tested before it went into operation, etc, etc.

The submariners were right: it was back to the drawing board. An embarrassed board of inquiry discovered that the firing pin at the nose of the torpedo had been breaking off before it could perform its rather simpleminded job.

The missile aimed at Kali impacted not at a trivial few kilometers an hour, but at more than a hundred kilometers *a second.* At such a velocity, a mechanical firing pin was useless: the warhead was moving many times faster than the news of contact, creeping at the speed of sound in metal, could convey its lethal message. Needless to say, the designers were perfectly well aware of this, and had used a purely electrical system to detonate the warhead.

They had a better excuse than the U.S. Navy's Bureau of Ordnance: it was impossible to test the system under realistic conditions.

So no one would ever know just why it failed to work.

45

THE
IMPOSSIBLE
SKY

IF THIS IS HEAVEN OR HELL, CAPTAIN ROBERT SINGH TOLD HIMself, it looks remarkably like my cabin aboard *Goliath*.

He was still trying to accept the unbelievable fact that he was still alive, when he received welcome confirmation from David.

"Hello, Bob—it wasn't easy to wake you."

"What—what's happened?"

No one had ever programmed David to hesitate like a human person: it was one of the many conversational tricks he had learned from experience.

"Frankly, I don't know. Obviously, the bomb failed to detonate. But something very strange has happened. I think you'd better get to the bridge."

Captain Singh, suddenly restored to his command, shook his head violently several times and was somewhat surprised to find that it remained attached to his shoulders. Everything appeared perfectly—incredibly—normal. He even felt a mild sense of annoyance, though hardly disappointment. It seemed an anticlimax to have wasted so much emotional energy coming to terms with Death—yet still be alive.

By the time he had reached the bridge, he had accepted the reality of the situation. His composure did not last for long.

The main view-screen still gave the illusion that there was nothing between him and the familiar landscape of Kali. That was unchanged; but what lay beyond it filled Captain Singh with one of the few moments of real terror he had ever known. Doubtless his peculiar emotional state was partly responsible: even so, no one could have looked at the sky above *Goliath* without an overwhelming sense of awe.

Looming above the steeply curved horizon of Kali, climbing perceptibly even as he watched, was the pockmarked landscape of another world. For a moment Robert Singh felt that he was back on Phobos, looking up at the gigantic face of Mars. But this apparition was even larger—and Mars, of course, was forever fixed in the sky of Phobos, not moving steadily toward the zenith, like this impossible object. *Or was it coming closer?* They had tried to stop one cosmic nomad falling upon the Earth: was another about to crash into Kali?

"Bob—Sir Colin wants to speak to you."

Singh had totally forgotten his companions: looking around, he was surprised to find that half the crew had joined him on the bridge, and were also staring in astonishment at the sky.

"Hello, Colin," he forced himself to say; it was not easy to talk to someone who should be dead. "What in God's name has happened?"

"Spectacular, isn't it?" The scientist's voice was calm and reassuring. "We had a grandstand view up here on the sled. Don't you recognize it? You should—you're looking at Kali! The bomb may have fizzled—but it still had megatons of kinetic energy. Enough to make Kali fission like an amoeba. Did a neat job too. Hope *Goliath* wasn't damaged; we'll need it as a home for a little while longer. But for *how* long? As Hamlet remarked, 'That is the question.' "

•   •   •

THE REUNION PARTY WAS MORE LIKE A THANKSGIVING SERVICE THAN a celebration: feelings ran too deep for that. From time to time the buzz of conversation in the wardroom would suddenly stop, and there would be complete silence while everyone shared a single thought: "Am I really alive—or am I dead and merely *dreaming* that I'm alive? And how long is the dream going to last?" Then somebody would crack a feeble joke, and the arguments and discussions would resume.

Most of them centered around Sir Colin, who, as he had claimed, had indeed enjoyed a grandstand view. The oncoming missile had hit near the asteroid's narrowest point—the waist of the peanut—but instead of the nuclear fireball the two watchers had anticipated, there had been a huge fountain of dust and debris. When it had cleared, Kali had seemed unchanged: then, very slowly, it split into two almost equal-size fragments. As each carried part of Kali's original spin, they then began a leisurely separation, like two whirling ice skaters who had let go of each other's hands.

"I've visited a half dozen twin asteroids," said Sir Colin, "starting with Apollo 4769—Castalia. But I never dreamed I'd see one being born! Of course, we won't have Kali 2 as a moon for very long—it's already drifting away. The big question is—will either of us hit the Earth? Or neither?

"With any luck, we'll both pass on either side—so even if that bomb didn't go off, it may have done its job. SPACE-GUARD should have the answer in a few hours. But if I were you, Sonny, I wouldn't take any bets on it."

46
FINALE

On *Goliath,* at least, the suspense did not last for long. SPACEGUARD was able to report almost immediately that Kali 1—the slightly smaller fragment on which the ship was stranded—would miss Earth by a comfortable margin. Captain Singh received the news with relief rather than elation: it seemed only fair, after all that they had endured. True, the Universe knew nothing of fairness: but one could always hope.

Goliath's orbit would be only slightly deflected as it raced past the Earth at several times escape velocity; then the ship and its little private world would continue to gain speed like a sun-grazing comet, dipping inside the orbit of Mercury at closest approach. The sheets of reflecting foil that Torin Fletcher was already assembling to form a giant tent would protect them from a heat load ten times that of a Saharan noon. As long as they kept their solar umbrella in good repair, they had nothing to fear except boredom: it would be more than three months before *Hercules* could catch up with them.

They were safe, and already belonged to History. But on Earth, no one knew whether History would continue: all that the SPACEGUARD computers could now guarantee was that Kali 2 would not make a direct impact on any major land-mass. That was some reassurance: but not enough to prevent mass panics, thousands of suicides, and partial breakdowns of law and order. Only the swift assumption of dictatorial pow-ers by the World Council prevented worse disasters.

The men and women aboard *Goliath* watched with concern and compassion, yet with a sense of detachment, almost as if they were looking at events that already belonged to the dis-tant past. Whatever happened to Earth, they knew that they would presently go their separate ways on their various worlds—forever marked by memories of Kali.

•   •   •

NOW THE HUGE CRESCENT OF THE MOON SPANNED THE SKY, THE jagged mountain peaks along the terminator burning with the fierce light of the lunar dawn. But the dusty plains still un-touched by the sun were not completely dark; they were glowing faintly in the light reflected from Earth's clouds and continents. And scattered here and there across that once-dead landscape were the glowing fireflies that marked the first permanent settlements mankind had built beyond the home planet; Captain Singh could easily locate Clavius Base, Port Armstrong, Plato City. . . . He could even see the necklace of faint lights along the Translunar Railroad, bringing its pre-cious cargo of water from the ice mines at the South Pole. And there was the Sinus Iridum, where he had achieved his first brief moment of fame a lifetime ago.

Earth was only two hours away.

Encounter Four

Kali 2 entered the atmosphere just before sunrise, a hundred kilometers above Hawaii. Instantly, the gigantic fireball brought a false dawn to the Pacific, awakening the wildlife on its myriad islands. But few humans; not many were asleep this night of nights, except those who had sought the oblivion of drugs.

Over New Zealand the heat of the orbiting furnace ignited forests and melted the snow on mountaintops, triggering avalanches into the valleys beneath. By great good fortune, the main thermal impact was on the Antarctic—the one continent that could best absorb it. Even Kali could not strip away all the kilometers of polar ice, but the Great Thaw would change coastlines all around the world.

No one who survived hearing it could ever describe the sound of Kali's passage; none of the recordings were more than feeble echoes. The video coverage, of course, was superb, and would be watched in awe for generations to come. But nothing could ever compare with the fearsome reality.

Two minutes after it had sliced into the atmosphere, Kali reentered space. Its closest approach to Earth had been sixty kilometers. In that two minutes it took a hundred thousand lives and did a trillion dollars' worth of damage.

•   •   •

THE HUMAN RACE HAD BEEN VERY, VERY LUCKY.

Next time it would be much better prepared. Though the encounter had altered Kali's orbit so drastically that it would never again be a danger to Earth, there were a billion other flying mountains orbiting the sun.

And Comet Swift-Tuttle was already accelerating toward perihelion. There was still plenty of time for it to change its mind again.

SOURCES AND
ACKNOWLEDGMENTS

MY INVOLVEMENT WITH THE SUBJECT OF ASTEROID IMPACTS IS NOW beginning to resemble a DNA molecule: the strands of fact and fiction are becoming inextricably entwined. Let me try to unravel them by taking the chronological approach.

Back in 1973 *Rendezvous with Rama* opened with the words:

> Sooner or later, it was bound to happen. On June 30, 1908, Moscow escaped destruction by three hours and four thousand kilometers—a margin invisibly small by the standards of the universe. On February 12, 1947, another Russian city had a still narrower escape, when the second great meteorite of the twentieth century detonated less than four hundred kilometers from Vladivostok, with an explosion rivaling that of the newly invented uranium bomb.

In those days there was nothing that men could do to protect themselves against the last random shots in the cosmic
bombardment that had once scarred the face of the Moon.
The meteorites of 1908 and 1947 had struck uninhabited wil-
derness; but by the end of the twenty-first century there was
no region left on Earth that could be safely used for celestial
target practice. The human race had spread from pole to pole.
And so, inevitably . . .

At 0946 GMT on the morning of September 11 in the ex-
ceptionally beautiful summer of the year 2077, most of the
inhabitants of Europe saw a dazzling fireball appear in the
eastern sky. Within seconds it was brighter than the sun, and
as it moved across the heavens—at first in utter silence—it left
behind it a churning column of dust and smoke.

Moving at fifty kilometers a second, a thousand tons of rock
and metal impacted on the plains of northern Italy, destroying
in a few flaming moments the labor of centuries. The cities of
Padua and Verona were wiped from the face of the Earth; and
the last glories of Venice sank forever beneath the seas as the
waters of the Adriatic came thundering landward after the
hammer blow from space.

Six hundred thousand people died, and the total damage
was more than a trillion dollars. But the loss to art, to history,
to science—to the whole human race, for the rest of time—
was beyond all computation. It was as if a great war had been
fought and lost in a single morning, and few could draw much
pleasure from the fact that, as the dust of destruction slowly
settled, for months the whole world witnessed the most
splendid dawns and sunsets since Krakatoa.

After the initial shock, mankind reacted with a determination and a unity that no earlier age could have shown. Such a
disaster, it was realized, might not occur again for a thousand
years—but it might occur tomorrow. And the next time the
consequences could be even worse.

Very well; there would be no next time.
So began Project Spaceguard.

Contrary to general belief, when I ended the novel with the words "The Ramans did everything in threes," I had not the slightest intention of writing a sequel, still less a trilogy. It seemed a neat ending, and was in fact an afterthought. It took the intervention of Peter Guber and Gentry Lee to make me change my mind (see the introduction to *Rama II*) and no one was more surprised than I to find myself revisiting Rama in 1986.

But by then something else had happened, making asteroid impacts front-page news. In a famous paper ("Extraterrestrial Cause for the Cretaceous-Tertiary Extinction": *Science,* 1980) Nobel Laureate Luis Alvarez and his geologist son, Dr. Walter Alvarez, had advanced a startling theory to explain the mysteriously sudden demise of the dinosaurs—perhaps the most successful life-form ever to arise on Planet Earth, next to sharks and cockroaches. As everyone now knows, the Alvarezes showed that a worldwide catastrophic event had occurred about sixty-five million years ago, and they produced evidence strongly suggesting that an asteroid was responsible. The direct impact, and the subsequent environmental damage, would have had a devastating effect on all terrestrial life—especially the larger land animals.

By a curious coincidence Luis Alvarez also had a major but fortunately beneficial impact upon *my* life. In 1941, as head of a team at MIT's Radiation Lab, he invented and developed the radar blind-landing system later known as GCA (ground controlled approach). The Royal Air Force—then losing more aircraft to the British weather than to the Luftwaffe—was extremely impressed by the demonstrations, and the first experimental unit was shipped to England in 1943. As an RAF radar officer, I had the fascinating, and often frustrating, job of keeping the Mark I operational until the first factory models rolled off the production line. My only non-sf novel, *Glide Path* (1963), is based on that experience, and is dedicated to "Luie" and his colleagues.

Luie left GCA shortly before I arrived, and flew over Hiroshima on that fateful August day in 1945 to observe the operation of the bomb he had helped design. I did not catch up with him until several years later, at the University of California's Berkeley campus; the last time we met was at the twenty-fifth GCA reunion in Boston, 1971. I am sorry that I never had a chance to discuss his dinosaur-extinction theory with him; in one of the last letters I received from him, he said it was no longer a theory but a fact.

Little more than a year before his death on September 1, 1988, Luie asked me to write a "puff" to be printed on the jacket of his forthcoming autobiography: *Alvarez: Adventures of a Physicist* (Basic Books, 1987). I was more than happy to do so, and would like to repeat what is now, alas, a posthumous tribute:

> Luis seems to have been there at most of the high points of modern physics—and responsible for many of them. His entertaining book covers so much ground that even nonscientists can enjoy it: who else has invented vital radar systems, hunted for magnetic monopoles at the South Pole, shot down UFOs and Kennedy assassination nuts, watched the first two atomic explosions from the air—and proved that (surprisingly) there are no hidden chambers or passageways inside Chephren's pyramid?
>
> And now he's engaged on his most spectacular piece of scientific detection, as he unravels the biggest whodunit of all time—the extinction of the dinosaurs. He and his son Walter are sure they've found the murder weapon in the Crime of the Eons. . . .

Since Luie's death, the evidence for at least one major meteor (or small asteroid) impact has accumulated, and several possible sites have been identified—the current favorite being a buried crater, 180 kilometers across, at Chicxulub, on the Yucatan Peninsula.

Some geologists are still fighting stubbornly for a purely terrestrial explanation of dinosaur extinction (e.g., volcanoes), and it may well turn out that there is truth in both hypotheses. But the Meteor Mafia appears to be winning, if only because its scenario is much the most dramatic.

In any case, no one doubts that major impacts have occurred in the past—after all, there have been two hits and one near miss in this century (Tunguska, 1908: Sikhote-Alin, 1947: Oregon, 1972). The question to be decided is: how serious is the danger, and what—if anything—can be done about it?

During the 1980s there was widespread discussion of the problem in the scientific community, and the close passage of asteroid 1989FC (which missed Earth by a mere 650,000 kilometers) brought the matter to a head. As a result, the U.S. House of Representatives Committee on Science, Space, and Technology included the following paragraph in the NASA Authorization Act of 1990:

> The Committee therefore directs that NASA undertake two workshop studies. The first would define a program for dramatically increasing the detection rate of Earth-orbit-crossing asteroids; this study would address the costs, schedule, technology, and equipment required for precise definition of the orbits of such bodies. The second study would define systems and technologies to alter the orbits of such asteroids or to destroy them if they should pose a danger to life on Earth. The Committee recommends international participation in these studies and suggests that they be conducted within a year of the passage of this legislation.

This may prove to be a historic document: who would have believed, only a few years ago, that a congressional committee would have issued such a statement?

As directed, NASA set up the International Near-Earth-Object Detection Workshop, which held several meetings in 1991. The results were summarized in a report prepared by the Jet Propulsion Laboratory, Pasadena: "The Spaceguard Survey" (January 25, 1992). The opening paragraph of its final chapter reads:

> Concern over the cosmic impact hazard motivated the U.S. Congress to request that NASA conduct a workshop to study ways to achieve a substantial acceleration in the discovery rate for near-Earth asteroids. This report outlines an international survey network of ground-based telescopes that could increase the monthly discovery rate of such asteroids from a few to as many as a thousand. Such a program would reduce the time scale required for a nearly complete census of large Earth-crossing asteroids from several centuries (at the current discovery rate) to about 25 years. We call this proposed survey program the Spaceguard Survey, borrowing the name from the similar project suggested by science-fiction author Arthur C. Clarke nearly 20 years ago in his novel *Rendezvous with Rama*.

The Hammer of God could not possibly have been written without the masses of information contained in "The Spaceguard Survey"—but the direct inspiration for the novel came from a quite different, and very unexpected, source.

In May 1992 I was flattered to receive a letter from Steve Koepp, senior editor of *Time* magazine, asking me to write a 4000-word story that would "give readers a snapshot of life on Earth in the next millennium." He added engagingly: "I believe it would be the first time that our magazine has ever published fiction (intentionally, at least)."

As it turned out, this information was not quite accurate. *Time*'s editors later informed me, rather apologetically, that mine was *not* the first fiction they had ever commissioned. Back in 1969 they had published a story by Aleksandr Solzhenitsyn. I am honored to follow in such distinguished footsteps.

Time's suggestion was, needless to say, an offer I couldn't refuse. It presented an interesting challenge, and I do not recall a delay of more than five milliseconds before I realized that the perfect subject was already at hand. More than that— it was my *duty* to show what could be done about the asteroid menace. By creating a self-fulfilling prophecy I might even save the world—though I'd never know. . . .

So I wrote *The Hammer of God* and rushed it off to *Time*, where Steve Koepp justified his existence by making some very shrewd editorial suggestions, 90 percent of which I accepted with (fairly) good grace. It appeared in the special issue of the magazine, *Beyond the Year 2000*, published in late September and dated Fall 1992 (Vol. 140, No. 27).

Before then, however, I had gone to England for the slightly premature celebrations of my seventy-fifth birthday (after three decades of living less than a thousand kilometers from the Equator, nothing will get me to the U.K. in December). Among the participants in the program that my brother Fred had arranged in my hometown, Minehead, was one of the members of the Spaceguard Survey, Dr. Duncan Steel. He had come all the way around the world, from the Anglo-Australian Observatory, Coonabarabran, NSW, to present a paper showing, with some awesome color slides, what might happen in the event of a major impact.

It was probably around this time that I accepted the fact that *Hammer* was really a compressed novel—and that I had no alternative but to decompress it. As I had six other books and several dozen TV programs in orbit, I was reluctant to bite this particular bullet, but eventually decided to cooperate with the inevitable.

The first draft was almost complete when I received a letter from Dr. Steel, now back in Coonabarabran, with some startling news:

Until last Thursday, if anyone had asked me when an asteroid or comet was going to collide with the Earth, I could have put my hand on my heart and told them that none of the currently-known objects is going to hit our planet in the foreseeable future (meaning a century or two). This is no longer the case. . . .

Attached to Dr. Steel's letter was Circular 5636, dated October 15, 1992, from the Central Bureau for Astronomical Telegrams, which is part of the Smithsonian Astrophysical Observatory, Cambridge, Massachusetts. It reported the rediscovery on September 26 of Comet Swift-Tuttle, originally discovered by two American astronomers in 1862—and then lost, not through carelessness but for a much more interesting reason.

When it nears the sun, Swift-Tuttle, like many comets (including Halley) undergoes solar-powered jet propulsion, the operation of which is completely unpredictable. Though the effect on its orbit is quite small, as Dr. Steel remarks: "If the sums and models are slightly incorrect—and one might not expect this jetting force to act consistently—then the comet may hit the Earth on August 14, 2126. There is no doubt about the *date,* since that is the date on which the comet's orbit intersects that of the Earth in that year; what is uncertain at this stage is whether the comet will be there at that time as well, or whether (hopefully) it will be slightly further on or back in its orbit."

Understandably, the Astronomical Union Circular suggests: "It therefore seems prudent to attempt to follow Swift-Tuttle for as long as possible after the present perihelion passage, in the hope that an adequate orbit determination . . . can be made."

Duncan Steel again: "What if the comet does hit the Earth in 2126? This will occur at a speed of 60 km/sec. The nucleus is about 5 km in size, so the kilotonnage released, according to my calculations, would be equivalent to 200 million megatons, or 10 billion times the Hiroshima bomb. If 5 km were its diameter rather than radius, divide those figures by eight. Still a big bang in anybody's language. Best wishes—Duncan."

Now, I had set the arrival of my hypothetical Kali around 2110—at which date the real world may be starting to agonize over Swift-Tuttle, only sixteen years ahead. So I was very happy to use this information to "add an air of verisimilitude to an otherwise bald and unconvincing narrative," as *The Mikado* puts it so neatly.

•   •   •

NOW, HERE IS SOMETHING THAT *NO ONE* IS GOING TO BELIEVE. . . .

I was still polishing this chapter when I switched on CNN (the exact time: 6:20 P.M., November 6, 1992, just two hours ago). Imagine my amazement at seeing my old friend the Dutch-American astronomer Tom Gehrels, expert on asteroids and a prominent member of the Spaceguard team. He has visited Sri Lanka on several occasions, hoping to establish an observatory there: his engaging autobiography, *On the Glassy Sea* (American Institute of Physics, 1988), has a chapter headed "Sri Lanka's Telescope and Arthur C. Clarke."

And what is Tom doing on CNN? He's just reporting the final confirmation of the Alvarez theory. The smoking gun has been found—and ground zero is, as I mentioned a few pages earlier, the Chicxulub structure in Yucatan.

Thank you, Tom: how I wish Luie were still around to hear the news.

•   •   •

ANOTHER ODD COINCIDENCE TOOK PLACE SOON AFTER *HAMMER* WAS published: a small meteorite landed in New York, of all places —damaging a parked car! (What else could it hit?) At least, that was the story I heard, but I am understandably skeptical. I cannot help wondering if *Time*'s publicity department was somehow involved. . . .

This incident, however, reminds me of the movie *Meteor*, which I enjoyed more than most of the critics. I have a very high threshold of tolerance for bad sf films. After persuading him to view one classic (*Things to Come,* I believe), Stanley Kubrick complained: "What are you trying to do to me? I'll never see another movie you recommend!"

There is a brilliant throwaway line at the climax of *Meteor*. After the bombardment from space, the Russian scientist and his American counterpart have just struggled back to the surface, having taken shelter in the New York subway. They are both covered with mud from head to foot. The Russian turns to his colleague and says: "Someday I must show you the Moscow Underground."

The rough riders of the IRT's graffiti-festooned cattle trucks would appreciate that wisecrack.

•   •   •

THE TUNGUSKA EVENT OF 1908 WAS FEATURED IN THE TV SERIES *ARthur C. Clarke's Mysterious World,* and a detailed discussion, with photographs and maps, will be found in Chapter 9 ("The Great Siberian Explosion") of the book by Simon Welfare and John Fairley.

•   •   •

MY COAUTHOR GREGORY BENFORD (*BEYOND THE FALL OF NIGHT*) HAS just reminded me of the novel he and William Rotsler wrote on the theme of asteroid deflection—*Shiva Descending* (1980). I must confess that I've never read it, but I was certainly aware of the title, and it may well have subconsciously influenced the choice of Kali (Shiva's consort) as the name for my asteroid. It popped into my head instantly when I started writing.

Another novel on the same theme is *Lucifer's Hammer* by Larry Niven and Jerry Pournelle (1980) which I *have* read—and which has just triggered a faint memory of dear old *Astounding Stories.* Rushing to Mike Ashby's invaluable *Complete Index to Astounding/Analog,* I've found the cause: "The Hammer of Thor," a short story by Charles Willard Diffin (March 1932).

I'm astonished—er, astounded—that I've recalled this obscure tale of space invaders, but it has obviously been lurking in my subconscious for the last sixty years. And to complete the record, I'm happy to admit that I quite deliberately stole my own very similar title from G. K. Chesterton. His priest-detective, Father Brown, solved a mysterious murder involving "The Hammer of God."

I should also mention the novel *A Torrent of Faces* by James Blish and Norman L. Knight (1967) which concerns the impact of an asteroid on an Earth with a population of a *trillion,* and the attempt to divert it. I cannot help feeling that such a world could do with an asteroid impact from time to time.

The Martian place-names mentioned in Chapter 14, improbable though they sound, are all taken from the NASA *Atlas of Mars* (1979). To spare readers the pangs of unrequited curiosity, here are their origins:

Dank: town in Oman; Dia-Cau: town in Vietnam; Eil: town in Somalia; Gagra: town in USSR (Georgia); Kagul: town in USSR (Moldavia); Surt: town in Libya; Tiwi: town in Oman; Waspam: town in Nicaragua; Yat: town in Nigeria.

I am currently trying to persuade the nomenclature committee of the International Astronomical Union to put Isaac Asimov, Robert Heinlein, and Gene Roddenberry on Mars. Unfortunately all the major formations have already been appropriated, so we may have to settle for Mercury—which, as my IAU contact wryly remarks, "may not be colonized for some time."

•   •   •

THE THEORETICAL BASIS OF THE REBORN DOCTRINE (CHAPTER 20) will be found in "Efficiently coded messages can transmit the information content of a human across interstellar space" by William A. Reupke, *Acta Astronautica,* Vol. 26, No. 3/4, pp. 273–76, March/April 1992.

NOTE ON MURPHY'S LAW (CHAPTER 44)

The almost unbelievable story of the United States Navy's torpedo failures, which took almost two years to rectify, will be found in *United States Submarine Operations in World War II* by Theodore Roscoe (U.S. Naval Institute, 1949) and more accessibly in *Coral Sea, Midway and Submarine Actions* by Samuel Eliot Morison (Little, Brown, 1959). To quote from the latter: "The firing pin, supposed to function under physical impact, proved too fragile to stand up under a good, square 90-degree hit. . . . Thus the best shooting was rewarded by duds."

ACKNOWLEDGMENTS

Apologies to Bob Singh, paragon of pill pushers, for borrowing his name in a fit of absentmindedness.

My thanks to Ray Bradbury for permission to use the quotation from *The Martian Chronicles* ("Night Meeting") in Chapter 24.

Special thanks to Prince Sultan al-Saud, Shuttle astronaut, for his hospitality at the Association of Space Explorers Meeting in Riyadh, November 1989, which gave me my first direct contact with Islamic culture.

And to Gentry Lee, for widening my technical and psychological horizons.

•   •   •

SPECIAL THANKS TO THE SUMMA CORPORATION FOR A MANGANESE nodule dredged up in 1972 from 16,500 feet, during the overture to the CIA's Operation Jennifer. (See *The Ghost from the Grand Banks.*) It looks so much like Kali that merely holding it in my hands often gave inspiration at arid moments.

•   •   •

PROGRAMS I FOUND OF GREAT VALUE DURING THE WRITING OF THIS book were VISTAPRO and DISTANT SUNS (Virtual Reality Laboratory, 2341 Ganador Court, San Luis Obispo, California 93401) for the AMIGA, and The Sky (Software Bisque, 912 Twelfth Street, Suite A, Golden, Colorado 80401) and Dance of the Planets (ARC Science Simulations, P.O. Box 1955S, Loveland, Colorado 80539) for MS/DOS. I am also grateful to Simon Tulloch for orbital calculations, though I may have occasionally repealed the law of inverse squares for dramatic purposes.

STOP PRESS. . . .

The manuscript of this novel was couriered to my US and UK agents on December 2, 1992. On December 8, the recently discovered asteroid Toutatis made its closest approach to Earth, a mere three million kilometers. Astronomers from the Jet Propulsion Laboratory took the opportunity to scan it with a new radar system at NASA's Mojave Desert station. They found that Toutatis consists of *two* heavily cratered bodies, between three and four kilometers in diameter, revolving about each other, almost in contact. The radar image shows an object exactly like Kali after it had split.

This is the first discovery of a double asteroid. Radar had shown Apollo 4769 (Castalia), referred to in Chapter 45, to be dumbbell shaped: quite probably, as I assumed, it is also a "contact binary."

• • •

THE LATEST (JANUARY 1, 1993) NEWS ON SWIFT-TUTTLE, RELAYED TO me by Dr. Duncan Steel, is that a better determination of its orbit makes a 2126 impact unlikely: it may miss Earth by fifteen days. But the last line of the novel still stands: and Dr. Steel adds ominously that fragments calving off the comet, as has been observed in several cases may yet present a hazard: "How do you fancy a hundred Tunguskas in a day?"